James bent and kissed her – hard

"Do you know what that is?" he asked her.

Clotilde took a steadying breath and did her best to behave normally, which was difficult in the circumstances. "No," she managed.

"That's my farewell salute to Sister Clotilde Collins." He grinned at her. "You can think about that until I see you again, Tilly."

He was gone — just like that, leaving the office door open. She wanted to shout a dozen questions at him. Did he know she was leaving? Probably the Principal Nursing Officer had told him.

Or was it, she wondered, an oblique way of telling her he had decided to marry Dr. Mary Evans after all?

Books by Betty Neels

HARLEQUIN ROMANCE

These books may be available at your local bookseller.

Don't miss any of our special offers. Write to us at the following address for information on our newest releases.

Harlequin Reader Service
P.O. Box 52040, Phoenix, AZ 85072-2040
Canadian address: P.O. Box 2800, Postal Station A,
5170 Yonge St., Willowdale, Ont. M2N 5T5

Once for All Time

Betty Neels

Harlequin Books

TORONTO • NEW YORK • LONDON
AMSTERDAM • PARIS • SYDNEY • HAMBURG
STOCKHOLM • ATHENS • TOKYO • MILAN

Original hardcover edition published in 1984
by Mills & Boon Limited

ISBN 0-373-02666-8

Harlequin Romance first edition January 1985

CHAPTER ONE

Women's Medical was quiet, for the Senior Consulting Physician's round had just begun. Dr Thackery was already at the first bed; a large man and tall, with lint-fair hair thickly sprinkled with grey, and blue heavy-lidded eyes. Oblivious of the admiring gaze of his patients fastened upon his handsome head, he bent over the elderly woman he was examining, his own gaze fixed on the wall behind her bed while he prodded gently.

Presently he said over his shoulder: 'Sister, I think we'll have another X-ray.' He had a deep deliberate voice, and his newly appointed House Physician drew in her breath at the sound of it and closed her eyes in a lovesick fashion. Clotilde handed over the appropriate form and gave her a quick amused glance as she did so. Everyone—that was, everyone female fell for Dr Thackery; such a silly waste of time too, because he was quite oblivious of their adoring looks. She had worked for him for three years now and never once had he cast an eye, even faintly interested, at any one of the nurses, sisters or women doctors working at St Alma's. He wasn't married, although he had been seen on numerous occasions with a variety of girls—and good luck to him, mused Clotilde, briskly handing the signed form to Dr Evans, who received it as though it were a gift from heaven, blushing heavily. He was nice, kind and thoughtful and almost annoyingly placid, although she had upon occasion felt acute pity for whoever he was hauling over the coals in that calm courteous voice, chilly with icy displeasure. But never with her; they enjoyed a pleasant relationship, a detached friendliness which was quite impersonal. Away from the ward she knew nothing about him, nor was she curious, and if he was to have called her Clotilde instead of Sister Collins she would have been dumbstruck. That he mostly looked at her as though he didn't see her properly didn't vex her in the least; she was a pretty girl with dark thickly fringed eyes, a straight nose and a wide curving mouth and hair as dark as her eyes, inclined to curl and which she screwed into a bun on top of her head, adding another inch or two to her tall and splendid figure. Possessed of these attributes, she had never lacked attention from men, and now that she and Bruce were engaged, she had little interest in anyone else.

Dr Thackery made his leisurely way to the next bed and she went with him, notes ready to hand, her mind now wholly on her work; which was more than could be said for Dr Evans, or, for that matter, his patient.

Miss Knapp was fiftyish, thin, refined and with a tongue as sharp as her equally sharp nose. But during Dr Thackery's round the sharpness was hidden under a die-away behaviour calculated to attract his sympathy.

Only it didn't. His manner towards her couldn't be faulted; Clotilde had to admit that his bedside manner was flawless, he had examined her, asked a few pertinent questions, assured her that she would be going home within a few days, and passed on to the next bed before she could squeeze out a single tear of self-pity.

A different kettle of fish here. Old Mrs Perch lay quietly, seldom speaking, and then only to thank someone for whatever they had done for her.

Leukaemia, held at bay by Dr Thackery for hard-fought months, was at last catching up with her; she knew it and so did he, but he sat on the edge of the bed, engaging her in cheerful talk between his questions, and was answered with equal cheerfulness. 'And this dear girl,' whispered Mrs Perch, nodding at Clotilde, 'always there when she's wanted—you have no idea what a treasure she is, Doctor.'

He dropped the lids over his eyes. 'Oh, but indeed I have, Mrs Perch. Sister Collins is my right hand, although I shall have to find myself another one when she marries.'

Mrs Perch chuckled, it sounded like paper rustling. 'There'll be plenty wanting to be that; you'll be able to take your pick, Doctor.' She glanced at Clotilde. 'I doubt you'll find her equal.'

'I doubt it too, Mrs Perch. And now I must bother you for a moment while Dr Evans takes some blood.'

He went to the end of the bed, listening to what his registrar, Jeff Saunders, had to say, half turned away from his patient. Which didn't prevent him seeing how Dr Evans fumbled so clumsily with the syringe that Clotilde took it gently from her, took the required amount of blood without fuss and handed it wordlessly back. He said nothing; it wasn't the first time Clotilde had given a helping hand. He stood impassively while Dr Evans transferred the blood to a test tube and then went back to his patient to bid her goodbye.

He was not to be hurried; Clotilde knew better than that. It was more than an hour by the time they had completed the round, and even then he paused at the end of the ward to discuss something with his Registrar. Clotilde thought longingly of her coffee and heaved a sigh of relief when he was at last finished and they

could go to her office. The little party broke up, the
social worker to go to her office, the radiographer to
the X-ray room, Staff Nurse Wood to see that the ward
was tidied and the patients comfortable and to send the
nurses to their coffee, and Dr Thackery, Jeff Saunders
and Dr Evans crowded into Clotilde's office where she
dispensed coffee and biscuits, offered bits of information
when asked for them and collected the pile of forms Dr
Thackery had signed. And all the while she listened
carefully to his instructions; he never gave her time to
write them down. She said: 'Yes, sir,' at intervals and
relied on her excellent memory.

Finally he had finished. The small party left her
office, crossed the landing and were ushered out into
the wide corridor connecting the men's and women's
medical blocks. Clotilde stood and watched them go,
Dr Thackery towering over his companions, his head a
little bent, deep in thought. He really needs a wife,
thought Clotilde, then wondered why on earth she had
thought that.

She spent the next hour with Sally Wood, making
notes, seeing that the right forms went to the right
departments, making sure that the instructions she had
received were passed on, and by the time that was done
the patients' dinners had arrived and they both went
into the ward and served the complicated diets suitable
for ulcers, heart failures, kidney disease and diabetes,
and that done, Clotilde left Sally to dish out the
puddings while she went from bed to bed, making sure
that the ladies under her care were eating their dinners,
listening patiently to complaints, encouraging poor
appetites, laughing at the jokes some of the convalescent
ladies were making in their cheerful Cockney voices.

She went to her own dinner then, with two of the

student nurses, leaving Sally and a second-year nurse to begin the business of settling everyone for their nap. But she didn't go straight to the dining room. Bruce would be in the entrance hall waiting for her. He was on the surgical side, one of Sir Oswald Jenkins' team, already marked out as a promising surgeon. She started down the last of the stairs and saw him standing with his back to her, talking to Sir Oswald. He was a little shorter than she was, dark-haired and good-looking, and Clotilde paused to admire him. He was ambitious, but she didn't hold that against him—indeed, when they married, her father had said he would buy him a practice as a wedding present, and Bruce had accepted without demur. Deep inside her she had been a little unhappy about that; foolishly so, she had told herself, for it was important to him to be successful. Sir Oswald had already hinted that he might be given a senior appointment at the hospital, and that, combined with a partnership in some well established practice, would be a splendid start.

She waited quietly until the two men had finished talking, and when Sir Oswald had been ushered out of the doors to his waiting car, she nipped down the last of the stairs. 'And what was all that about?' she wanted to know, and was a little taken aback by Bruce's quick frown.

'Nothing much, just general chat.' The frown had gone and he smiled at her. 'Had a good morning? Old Thackery's round, wasn't it?'

Clotilde nodded. 'He's an easy man to work for. He's got a new house doctor—Mary Evans—she's Welsh and head over heels already. You'd think he'd notice, but he really doesn't. I daresay he's got a girl somewhere or other and that makes him immune . . .'

Bruce said rather impatiently: 'Must we waste time talking about him?' And then: 'Has he ever made a pass at you, Tilly?'

She gave him a look of utter astonishment. 'Heavens above, no! What an idea. Whatever made you think of that?'

He shrugged his shoulders. 'Well, you're a pretty girl . . .'

She dimpled at him. 'Why, thank you, Bruce.' She smiled, her lovely eyes on a level with his, and at that moment Dr Thackery sauntered out of a passage and into the entrance. He passed them with a placid greeting and went through the glass double doors, and they both turned their heads to watch him.

'Lucky devil,' observed Bruce, 'driving a Bentley—he must be making a packet.'

Clotilde, watching Dr Thackery driving away with the minimum of fuss, said thoughtfully: 'Possibly he is, but he works hard and he's so nice to his patients.'

Bruce said sourly: 'He can afford to be; I expect his waiting room in Harley Street is packed with rich old ladies.'

Clotilde said bracingly: 'Well, my dear, probably in ten years' time you'll be doing exactly as he is doing now.' She sighed soundlessly, for Bruce did harp rather too much on the financial success of his future and not enough on the satisfaction of being a good surgeon. After all, he would be able to earn quite enough to keep them in comfort, and she didn't expect more. Her father, a retired Army man, had always had enough; they had lived in the nice old house in Essex, she and her parents and her elder sister, married now and living in Canada, and she went home regularly to Wendens Ambo, sometimes with Bruce, sometimes alone, although she was going to miss that for a while, as they had left only a week ago to drive to Switzerland. Standing there watching the faint discontent on Bruce's face, she thought she might go home for her days off, just to make sure that everything was all right. And if Bruce would come with her, so much the better; it might serve to remind him that he wasn't marrying a girl without expectations. After all, her father had made them the handsome offer of a partnership, and surely after the first stepping stone, Bruce would shoot ahead.

'I must go,' she said. 'Are we doing anything this evening? I'm off at five o'clock.'

'I'm free around six—we'll have a drink somewhere, shall we? I'm on call for the next two nights.'

'I'll have days off—I'll go home, I think and see if Rosie's all right.' Rosie was elderly and had been with her parents ever since she could remember. 'Mother and Father don't expect to be back for another two weeks.'

They parted quickly and Clotilde, already very late, hurried back to the dining room, where she joined her friends at the table set aside for sisters and ate the shepherd's pie put before her while discussing the morning's work.

'What did you do to upset our James Thackery?' asked Fiona Walters, sister on Men's Medical. 'Very terse this morning, in a placid way. Though I daresay it's that new house doctor mooning over him.

'She'll get over it,' observed Clotilde comfortably 'they all do in time, after all, he never encourages them.' 'men don't like to be chased', declared a small dark girl at the end of the table. Mary Evans was the acknowledged chaser in St Alma's and the table erupted in laughter.

Clotilde went home two days later. She hadn't seen

Bruce since their few hours together in the evening, but she hadn't expected to. He had no time to himself when he was on call; it was a state of affairs to which she had become accustomed. She drove herself, leaving early in the morning. The sky was dull and grey and it wasn't quite light, because there was a touch of winter about October already, but the traffic wasn't too heavy and she pushed the Mini ahead, making for the A11. Once clear of the city traffic and with Epping behind her, she sent the little car along at a good speed. She would be home in time for coffee for the journey was less than fifty miles. She and Rosie would sit at the kitchen table and gossip, then while her lunch was cooking she would take Tinker, the old retriever, for a walk. There had been a card from her mother the previous evening. Clotilde smiled, thinking of the ecstatic remarks about the Swiss Lakes, and the wonderful time they were having. She would have to see that she had days off when they got home so that she could be there with Rosie to welcome them.

She was through Bishop's Stortford by now, nearing the turning to Wendens Ambo. Saffron Walden was only two miles further on; perhaps she would go there tomorrow and have a look for a dress, something pretty for the occasional evening out she spent with Bruce.

The village, even under a grey sky, looked charming. Most of the cottages were whitewashed and thatched, their small gardens full of chrysanthemums and last snapdragons and roses. Clotilde turned off the lane to the church and went slowly along an even narrower lane and then through an open gateway, to stop before a fair-sized house, whitewashed too but with a lovely tiled roof and a handful of outbuildings. She got out of the car, to be greeted by a delighted Tinker and then by

Rosie, throwing open the door, already talking. Coffee wouldn't be a minute, and what a lovely surprise, and had Clotilde heard from her mother and father?

'I had a card this morning,' Rosie declared, leading the way indoors. 'Having a lovely time, by all accounts, but it'll be nice to have them back. You'll stay the night?'

'Two,' said Clotilde contentedly. 'I'm not on until one o'clock, so I can go up in the morning after breakfast. Rosie, its lovely to be home, and I'm famished!'

She put her things down on the oak settle in the hall and followed Rosie into the kitchen, where for the next hour they sat gossiping.

'And when will you marry, Miss Tilly?' asked Rosie at length.

'As soon as Bruce can find the practice he likes.' Clotilde frowned a little. 'The thing is to find the right one—it's got to be in a good neighbourhood you see.'

Bruce was adamant about that; how else was he going to be successful as a surgeon? he had wanted to know reasonably, after he had rejected several partnerships in small suburban practices; he had no intention of filling his days with run-of-the-mill patients on the N.H.S. Sir Oswald was the senior in a large partnership; it would be wonderful if he were to offer Bruce a job, thought Clotilde wistfully. She sometimes wondered if that was what Bruce was hoping for. He had turned down one or two quite good partnerships which would have enabled them to marry. His excuses had been flimsy ones and Clotilde had argued hotly with him each time. He had smoothed her down, though, and made her see how sensible he was being.

She passed her mug for more coffee and twisted the

diamond ring on her finger. It was a solitaire, not big, but good. When they had bought it Bruce had said laughingly that it had to be presentable so that when he was established as a well known consultant surgeon, she wouldn't need to feel ashamed of it. Clotilde, who wasn't keen on diamonds, chose the ring he pointed out. It was impossible to tell him that she would never be ashamed of his ring, even if it was brass and glass.

She drank her coffee, helped to tidy away the mugs and went up to her room. It was a pretty place, furnished with an assortment of furniture she had chosen for herself years ago—a small brass bedstead, a dressing table of yew and a triple mirror she had discovered in the attics. The small crinoline chair had come from the attics too, and her mother had had it upholstered in the same chintz which covered the bed and draped the window. Everything was a little shabby now after so many years, but the furniture shone with Rosie's vigorous polishing and the carpet, worn in places, was an original Moorfields. She put away the few things in her overnight bag, brushed her hair in a perfunctory fashion, and went downstairs, to whistle Tinker, call to Rosie that she was going for a walk, and leave the garden by the wicket gate in the high stone wall which separated it from the fields beyond.

There was a thin mist shrouding the distance and the grass was damp underfoot, but it was heaven after the narrow crowded streets round St Alma's. Clotilde took the footpath away from the village and then circled round to return past the church, call at the stores to buy the chocolate Rosie loved, and go back home to steak and kidney pudding and lashings of vegetables, followed by one of Rosie's treacle tarts.

'I'll get fat,' smiled Clotilde contentedly.

'A great strapping girl like you, Miss Tilly? There's enough of you to carry a few pounds more. Your dear ma always wanted to be a big girl.'

'Oh, well, she had me instead; goodness knows I'm big enough for the two of us. Rosie, when we've washed up I'm going into Saffron Walden. Do you want to come? And if you don't, is there anything you want?'

'Some more of that wool I'm using for my niece's sweater. I'll put my feet up while you're gone and we'll have a nice tea when you get back.'

Saffron Walden was bustling in a gentle way. Clotilde parked the car, bought the wool and then did a little shopping on her own account—tights and toothpaste and make-up and a crêpe blouse which would go rather well with the velvet skirt she sometimes wore when she and Bruce went out for the evening. She searched, not very hard, for a dress and then decided that she would wait until she went shopping in London, then since the dull day was fast turning into a thickening twilight, she drove back home to eat Rosie's scones round the fire in the comfortable sitting room. Rosie hadn't wanted to share her tea, she was old-fashioned and had strong views about keeping her place, but Clotilde wheedled her into the sitting room into the chair opposite hers and switched on the TV. There she ate almost all the scones and encouraged Rosie to talk about her youth, while Tinker lay with his head across her feet. She hadn't felt so content and happy for a long time. St Alma's seemed to be in another world, even Bruce seemed a vague figure, an outsider in the cosiness of the room. Nonsense, of course, she told herself briskly. He was very much part of her life, and when they were married they would come to her home together and sit round the fire and eat scones and talk . . .

'A nice cheese omelette for your supper,' Rosie's voice stopped her dreaming, 'and there's a trifle. It's nice to have someone to cook for.'

'You're spoiling me, Rosie. I hope you cook for yourself when you're here alone.'

'Course I do—and your ma told me to have Mrs Grimshaw from the Post Office up for supper whenever I want to.'

Clotilde woke the next morning to the smell of frying bacon and it was so tantalising that she got up at once, dressed in an elderly pleated skirt and a jersey and went down to the kitchen. Rosie looked up from the Aga.

'I guessed that would bring you down smart like, Miss Tilly—just you sit down and we'll have breakfast.' She opened the door and Tinker came rushing in, damp from the drizzle outside. 'Not much of a day,' she added.

'I'm going for a walk anyway,' declared Clotilde. 'I'll go down to Audley End and cross the park, then come home through the woods. It'll be good for Tinker.'

It took her the best part of the morning, but she didn't care. She made easy work of the miles, not bothering about the steady drizzle, and coming back through the village she met several people she knew and stopped to chat. She got back with a fine colour and a good appetite, dried Tinker, tidied herself and ate the dinner Rosie had ready. And afterwards she did the ironing, saw to the plants in the conservatory built on to the back of the house and then retired to the sitting room fire to read while Rosie had her nap on her bed. Later, going to bed, she thought happily that it had been a lovely day, no hustle or bustle, no Miss Knapp constantly complaining, no phone calls, no rounds. For no reason at all she found herself thinking about Dr

Thackery; he would be a pleasant companion with whom to walk in the rain. She suddenly was brought up short, feeling disloyal to Bruce, who hated rain anyway.

She said goodbye to Rosie and Tinker with regret the next morning. 'But I'll be back next week,' she told them. 'Mother and Father will be back on Thursday, won't they? I won't be able to get away before two o'clock, but they won't be home much before tea time. I'll bring some flowers with me.'

She waved goodbye and shot into the lane and through the village on her way back to St Alma's. She had hung about, talking to Rosie, and if she didn't hurry she would be late on duty. A nuisance; she had intended to go to the Surgical Wing first in case Bruce was there. Now she wouldn't have the time.

There was barely twenty minutes left as she turned into the hospital forecourt. She ran the Mini round the side of the sprawling building and parked it, and as she got out Dr Thackery's Bentley slid silently into the next parking lot. He should have parked in the consultants' reserved spaces and at her look of surprise, he said: 'I'm in a hurry and this is nearer. Have you had a pleasant time?'

'Yes, lovely.' She smiled at him. 'I'm late,' she told him.

'Then for heaven's sake don't let me keep you.' He spoke in his usual friendly fashion and turned to get his bag out of the car. But Clotilde paused to look in at the rear window at the Jack Russell sitting in the centre of the back seat. 'Is he yours?' she asked.

'Yes, and he's a she—Millie. She cadged a ride at the last minute.'

She smiled widely. 'She's rather gorgeous. You look as though you ought to have a Great Dane.'

His firm mouth twitched. 'But I have. His name is George, and he's car-sick.'

Clotilde gave a delighted chortle and then remembered the time. 'I must fly!' she exclaimed.

She was racing for the side door leading to the Nurses' Home when she bumped into Bruce, but before she could speak he said crossly: 'What was all that about? I've been standing here ...'

She pulled up short. 'Oh, Bruce, I'm so sorry—I was admiring Dr Thackery's dog. A Jack Russell ... I didn't see you.' She added unnecessarily: 'I'm late.'

'Then you'd better get a move on,' said Bruce loftily.

Not the best start to the rest of the day, thought Clotilde, tearing off her suit and getting into uniform. Now she would have to try and see Bruce that evening—hours away. But by then he might have forgotten about it, and after all, she told herself reasonably, one didn't ignore someone one worked with, especially someone as goodnatured as Dr Thackery.

The afternoon was busier than she would have liked, with two emergency admissions, Miss Knapp choosing to have an attack of hysterics just as teas were being served, and Miss Fitch next to her going into a diabetic coma. Not the easiest of days, thought Clotilde, drinking a hasty cup of tea in her office before starting on the medicine round, and to crown it all Dr Evans had been on the ward, throwing her weight around, annoying both nurses and patients. Usually Clotilde had found the women doctors easy to get on with; they cheerfully looked after themselves if they saw that the nurses were busy, but Dr Evans had had other ideas. She insisted on having someone in attendance, and that in the middle of the bedpan round ...

Clotilde went off duty at last tired and irritable, glad that the day was over. She gobbled her supper in the company of those of her friends who had just come off duty, then she went down to the lodge to see if Bruce had left a message. Old Diggs the porter looked up from his paper.

'Dr Johnson said he'll be free at half past nine and you was to go for a drink together.'

'Thanks, Diggs.' She felt suddenly much better; it would be late before she got to bed, but that would be a small price to pay for an hour of Bruce's company. She went back to her room and changed into a dress, and since it was damp and dreary outside, a raincoat. There was no point in dressing up; the local pub was used by almost everyone at the hospital and it was so near that all one needed to do was slip on a coat or a mac.

Clotilde was prompt and it was five minutes before Bruce arrived—and not in too good a temper, she saw, her heart sinking.

'Hallo.' His greeting was abrupt. 'A pity you've not bothered to get into something decent, now we'll have to go to the Lamb and Thistle, I suppose.'

'It's a bit late . . .' She didn't know why he was in a bad temper; too much to do, probably. A drink and a quiet chat should put that right.

But it didn't; he was edgy and ill at ease until she said forthrightly: 'What's the matter, Bruce? Had a bad day?'

'Nothing's the matter.' He covered her hand with his and gave it a squeeze. 'And the day was no worse than others. I had a long talk with Sir Oswald—he's offered me a junior partnership.'

'But that's marvellous Bruce, absolutely wonderful—I can't believe it! Of course you accepted?'

He shrugged. 'How can I? I'd have to buy myself in.' He mentioned a sum which sent her dark brows up.

'But that's twice what Father said he'd give us, and I don't honestly think that he could manage any more. Do you know anyone who'd lend it to you?'

'Yes, as a matter of fact, I do—at least, I'd have to do it through someone I know.'

'Not moneylenders?' asked Clotilde sharply, and got laughed at for her pains.

'Silly darling—no, of course not, and I won't do anything until I've talked to your father. He might be able to manage.'

'I'm sure he can't. He never talks about money, but I heard him talking to Mother about some shares that had dropped and he sounded worried.'

'Well, it can't be as bad as all that.' Bruce sounded uninterested. 'They've gone on holiday, haven't they, and the house isn't kept going on peanuts.'

He began to talk about his day and Clotilde, who would have liked to have made plans for their wedding, listened cheerfully. She wasn't tired any more; it was splendid news that Bruce had been offered a partnership with Sir Oswald—something he had always wanted. She had wanted it too, of course; it made their future together a good deal nearer, and after all, she was twenty-five, almost twenty-six, and Bruce was thirty. They went back presently and parted in the entrance hall. Even though there was no one there, only old Diggs, they didn't kiss. Bruce had said it was a bad example for the students.

They barely saw each other for the next couple of days. Clotilde had to be content with a quick wave from a distance and a note left at the lodge telling her that he was too busy to meet her. She accepted it more or less cheerfully; his work came first and when he was free he would be too tired to want to go out. She washed her hair, did her nails and went to the cinema with some of her friends. Bruce had said he would be free on the following day and she assumed that they would spend as much of it together as they could manage. It was Dr Thackery's round in the morning, but she had given herself a half day and she would be free after dinner.

The round went smoothly. Clotilde was ready and waiting, with Sally beside her, loaded with case notes and X-rays, when the ward doors were opened and Dr Thackery, hedged about by Jeff Saunders, the Evans woman and the rest of them, came into the ward. His 'good morning' was pleasant, impersonal and brisk and Clotilde was equally brisk. After the few years they had worked together, they appreciated the fine line they had drawn together between friendship and getting on with the job. Miss Knapp was dealt with with smooth competence and a quite definite decision that she might go home on the next day, the emergency cases which had been admitted during the week were examined at some length and Mrs Perch, almost at her last breath now, was gently teased and chatted to, just as though Dr Thackery had no other patients to see.

Presently they moved on to the next bed—Mrs Butler, a mountain of a woman, propped up in bed against her pillows, puffing her way through an asthmatic attack. She took a great deal of time too, and Clotilde felt a twinge of impatience. Her delightful nose had caught the first whiff of dinners; they would never be finished on time—which meant that she would be late off duty and Bruce would have to hang around . . .

An urgent tap on her sleeve broke her train of thought. Clare, the ward clerk, gave her a scared look because no one was supposed to interrupt the round. She stood on tiptoe to reach Clotilde's ear. 'There's a phone call for you in the Office, Sister. Urgent—they wouldn't give a message.'

'Did they gave their name?' Clotilde's whisper was almost soundless.

Clare looked helpless. 'I didn't ask, Sister.'

'It might be as well if you dealt with the matter yourself,' said Dr Thackery suddenly. 'We're almost finished, aren't we?'

He looked round and smiled at her and she found herself smiling back at him, even while she deplored his eavesdropping. She nodded to Sally to take her place and hurried down the ward. It would be anxious relations of one of the patients, she had no doubt. It was a favourite ploy to ring and say it was urgent and not give a name, because that made it necessary for her to go to the phone herself instead of letting the ward clerk deal with it. She lifted the receiver and said, 'Hullo?' then because there were sounds of distress at the other end, she added encouragingly: 'This is Sister Collins.'

Rosie's voice sounded in her ear—a voice thick with tears and distress. 'Miss Tilly—oh, Miss Tilly, however am I going to tell you? Your dear ma and pa . . .'

Clotilde felt her insides go cold. She asked in a rigidly controlled voice: 'There's been an accident, Rosie—where are they?'

'Oh, Miss Tilly, they've been killed! In a car crash in France, on their way home. The police came,' and then in a bewildered voice: 'What am I to do?'

Clotilde felt the ice inside her spreading, her arms felt leaden, her face stiff and her brain frozen solid. She said carefully: 'Don't worry, Rosie, I'll come home and see to everything.' After a pause she added: 'You're quite sure, aren't you, Rosie?'

'Yes, Miss Tilly. Will you be long?'

'No, a couple of hours, perhaps less.'

She put the receiver down carefully and sat down behind her desk. There was a lot to do, but just for the moment she was quite incapable of doing it.

It was ten minutes or more before Dr Thackery and his entourage reached her office. He opened the door, glanced at her frozen, ashen face, and turned round so that his bulk filled the doorway.

'I believe Sister has had bad news,' he said quietly. He nodded to his registrar. 'Start the round on the Men's Medical side will you? Staff Nurse, take over for the moment, will you, and bring some brandy here as quickly as you can.'

He didn't wait for them to answer but went into the office again, shutting the door after him.

Clotilde hardly noticed him, but when he came close and sat on the edge of the desk in front of her chair and took her icy hands in his she said politely: 'So sorry I didn't finish the round, but I—I've had some bad news.' She took a deep breath. 'My parents have been killed, somewhere in France—they were on their way home from Switzerland. They go most years because Mother likes it there.'

The hands holding hers tightened. 'My poor girl!' Dr Thackery's voice was very gentle, he went on holding her hands and when Sally came in with the brandy, nodded to her without speaking. When she had gone he picked up the glass. 'You're going to drink this because you need it,' and like a child she did so, coughing and spluttering and catching her breath, but there was a little colour in her cheeks now.

'That's better. You want to go home, of course? We'll settle that first.' He didn't let go of her hands, but dialled the Nursing Supervisor and presently put down the receiver. 'That's settled,' he told her. 'You can go home as soon as you want to. You have a car? Not that you're in a fit state to drive. Is Johnson free?'

And when she nodded he picked up the phone again. Clotilde, her shocked mind dulled by the brandy, only half listened; it sounded as though there was some difficulty. She leaned forward suddenly and said: 'Let me,' and took the receiver from Dr Thackery. Her voice sounded odd but it was almost steady. 'Bruce, I've had some bad news about—about Mother and Father. Would you drive me home?' She added tonelessly: 'They've been killed.'

His voice came over the wire very clearly. 'I say, I am sorry—how simply frightful! Of course you must go home straight away. The thing is I simply can't get away . . .' and when she interrupted with: 'But you're free today,' he went on: 'Yes, I know, but Sir Oswald's asked me to lunch and I simply must go—it's my whole future. I'll come down just as soon as I can afterwards. Why don't you go and lie down for a bit—get someone to give you a sedative. You'll feel more able to cope and later on we can get things sorted out.'

She didn't speak, only gave the receiver back to Dr Thackery, her face stony and whiter than ever. She said: 'I'll be quite all right to drive myself. Bruce can't manage . . .' She stopped and looked at him from huge dark eyes. 'He's having lunch with Sir Oswald,' she told him.

Dr Thackery said nothing at all to this, only gave her the rest of the brandy to drink and picked up the phone again. When he put it down he said with calm authority: 'Home Sister is coming here for you, you will go to your room with her and pack a bag.' He glanced at his watch. 'I'll be at the front entrance in twenty minutes. I'll drive you home.'

The brandy had made Clotilde feel peculiar, numb and still unable to think. She stared back at him and nodded obediently.

CHAPTER TWO

THINKING about it afterwards, Clotilde could remember very little of the drive to Wendens Ambo. Dr Thackery had spoken seldom and then in a calm matter-of-fact voice which had hardly penetrated her bewildered thoughts. They weren't really thoughts, anyway, just odds and ends of ideas which came to the surface and vanished again. Once when she thought of it she said: 'I didn't tell Staff about Mrs Perch's daughter . . .' and he had answered at once: 'I'll take back any messages you want to send,' and she had thought: Anyone else would have told me not to worry—like Home Sister, who had helped her pack her case and given her tea to drink and told her over and over again not to worry.

Rosie met them at the door, her nice elderly face puffed with weeping. She gave Clotilde a worried look and then glanced at the doctor.

'Rosie—I may call you that?—would you make a pot of tea? Then we'll sit down and talk, shall we?' And when she nodded, thankful to have someone to tell her what do do, and opened the sitting room door, he took Clotilde's elbow and ushered her into the room.

Perhaps it was the sight of her mother's work basket, standing on her little table, a piece of tapestry hanging from it, or the row of silver cups her father had won at various sports in his youth, which melted the ice inside her. Suddenly she was in floods of tears, her head resting on Dr Thackery's enormous chest, his arms holding her close. She cried for a long time. Rosie came in with the tray of tea and sat down quietly at a look from him, and only the phone ringing stopped her. Dr Thackery made no haste to answer it. He mopped Clotilde's eyes for her, sat her down in an easy chair and went into the hall to answer it.

'The police, wanting to know who will take care of things,' he told her, and handed her a cup and saucer. 'Drink up, there's a good girl.' He sat down near her, smiled at Rosie and started on his own tea. 'This has to be talked about,' he said gently, 'and you will feel better when you do. Have you a brother, uncle or anyone else in the family who can deal with the formalities?' And at Clotilde's blank look: 'Someone who can go over to France, identify your parents and arrange for them to be brought back here?'

Clotilde said in a tear-sodden voice: 'I've an older sister; she's married and lives in Canada and she's expecting another baby in two weeks' time. I've no uncles or cousins, and my godfather died last year.'

'What about young Johnson? I imagine the authorities would allow him to cope with the necessary arrangements.'

She remembered Bruce's voice—sympathetic but anxious not to be involved in anything which might spoil his chances with Sir Oswald. 'He's—he's got his job, I don't suppose he could get leave. Besides, he's assisting Sir Oswald all next week while the Senior Registrar's away.'

'Ah yes,' Dr Thackery's voice was dry, 'that makes it impossible for him to get away, doesn't it? I wonder if I would do. I didn't know your parents, but I imagine that your solicitor or even the local parson would come with me. I could make all the arrangements necessary for their return while you attend to matters at this end.'

He didn't wait for her to answer but went on in the same matter-of-fact voice: 'Now, there are several people to inform, aren't there? Your solicitor, the parson, your sister—perhaps it would be best to tell her husband and he could decide if she is to be told? I'll arrange for you to have leave from the hospital, and if you feel you can, write to Sally Wood and give her any instructions which might help her.'

He looked across the room at Rosie. 'I'm sorry I shall have to leave you quite soon. Eat something, the pair of you, and then lie down for an hour or so. Before I go I'll do some phoning, if I may. I'll need some phone numbers.'

It was Clotilde who got up and fetched the telephone book for him. She felt curiously empty and tired. The shock was beginning to wear off now and she was aware of the sharp edge of pain. She said: 'Do you have to go?'

'Yes, but I shall be back this evening. Can you put me up for the night? I'll be fairly late, I'm afraid.'

Rosie said eagerly: 'You'll want your supper, doctor. I'll see and cook you something.'

'That would be kind, but don't stay up for me. Something kept hot on the stove will suit me very well.' His blue eyes studied Clotilde from under their lids. 'If I might suggest that you both go to bed? I expect you leave the key under the mat?'

Clotilde nodded. 'Everyone does. But you don't need to come back, really you don't. You've been so kind and helpful—you've done too much already. We'll be quite all right.'

He only smiled gently, got up and went away to the telephone. Presently he came back. 'Your vicar will be round very shortly and your solicitor will be down to see you in the morning. Remember what I said and have a rest after lunch.' He bent and kissed Rosie's cheek, and at the door turned to kiss Clotilde too. 'Look after each other,' he said gravely. 'I'll see you, and I can let myself out.'

'What a nice gentleman,' said Rosie, 'doing all that for us too—and him no more than someone at the hospital. What happened to Mr Johnson?'

'He couldn't get away.' Clotilde busied herself putting the cups and saucers back on the tray. 'Rosie, I can't believe it, but we've got to go on as usual, haven't we? I'll go and make up a bed for Dr Thackery while you do something for lunch. I'm not hungry and I don't suppose you are either, but he said we must have something.'

Rosie was crying again, and she went and put her arms round the dear soul. 'Rosie, don't, please don't! The next few days are going to be awful and we've got to get through them somehow.' She kissed her and Rosie said between sobs:

'He kissed me too—so natural like, just as though he was a friend and really minded.'

'I think he does mind. He's always kind to his patients, and calm and quiet.' Clotilde added thoughtfully: 'But I don't know what he's really like.'

She made herself busy until the vicar came—an old man, and very shaken by the news. She gave him a glass of sherry because he looked as though he needed it, then poured one for Rosie and another for herself.

'Your friend has everything in hand', observed the vicar. 'You are most fortunate to have someone so helpful at such a sad time.' He added inevitably: 'Is Mr Johnson not with you?'

'He's unable to leave the hospital.' Clotilde was filled with fresh unhappiness. The one person who could have consoled her wasn't there. And he couldn't help it, she reminded herself—an important engagement with Sir Oswald just couldn't be missed; his future depended upon pleasing the great man. It wasn't as if Bruce had known her parents well. They had met on countless occasions, but in all fairness there was only a mild affection between them. A tiny voice reminded her that Dr Thackery hadn't known them at all, yet he was prepared to go to France for her.

She listened politely to the vicar making tentative arrangements and offering help. 'The village will be shocked,' he told her. 'Your parents were well liked. You will stay on here, of course? We would not like to see you go.'

'I hadn't thought about it,' said Clotilde, 'but I expect Rosie and I will go on living here, at least until I marry. We'll have to think about that later.'

He went away presently and she and Rosie had their lunch, sitting at the kitchen table, not talking much and not eating much either. They washed up together and then, obedient to the Doctor's instructions, went and lay down, and surprisingly, slept.

They had tea, then Rosie busied herself making soup to keep hot on the stove and a caramel custard to follow it. 'Because I'll be bound he'll be hungry when he gets here.' She asked hesitantly: 'When will he go to France, Miss Tilly?'

'I don't know, he'll tell us, though.' Clotilde went to answer the phone yet again; the news had got around and people were ringing up all the time.

They had their supper quite early and then because they couldn't bear to talk anymore, said goodnight and went to their rooms. Clotilde didn't undress at once but sat at her window, looking out on to the dark evening, not even thinking. It was much later when she got to her feet, cold now, and went to run a bath. She could hear Rosie snoring and uttered a thankful sigh; the poor dear had had a shock and she must be worn out with grief. She would have to go to bed herself, she supposed, and she took as long as possible undressing and bathing, brushing her long hair for ten minutes or more before at last getting into bed. It surprised her to see that it was already almost eleven o'clock. She was still making up her mind to put out the light when she heard the Bentley surge almost silently up to the front door. She had been dreading the moment when she must lie in the dark and try and sleep, now she seized on the chance to put that moment off till later. She got up, put on a dressing gown and slippers, and went silently downstairs.

Dr Thackery was in the kitchen, a saucepan lid in one hand, eyeing the soup. He looked up as she went in, said 'Hullo' in an unsurprised voice and then: 'How about sharing some of this soup with me? I dislike eating alone.'

Clotilde came slowly into the kitchen, her face puffy with weeping, her hair hanging in a curtain down her back, her nose pink. All the same, she still looked quite lovely.

'You didn't eat your supper.' He wasn't asking, just stating a fact, and she said quickly: 'We did try, really we did.'

He turned and fetched two bowls from the dresser and added them to the neatly laid tray Rosie had left ready, while Clotilde went to the bread bin and got out a loaf and sliced some bread.

'Have you been busy?' she asked.

'Yes, I saw Sally, and she sent a great many kind

messages and you're not to worry about a thing; she's been sent extra help until you get back and all the patients are okay She won't bother you with phoning, but if you want to ring her, she'd like that very much.'

They ate in silence for a minute or two and presently he went on: 'I'm going over to France tomorrow. I should be back in a couple of days at the latest. I've arranged things with the undertakers.' He mentioned the name of a firm in the nearest town. 'That's all you need to know at present, I think. As soon as you feel that you can and you want to, you can take over.'

Clotilde got up and fetched the coffee from the stove and put the soup bowls into the sink. There was one of Rosie's bacon and cheese flans on the table and she pushed it towards him. 'Please have some, you must be hungry. I can't thank you enough for all you're doing . . .'

He smiled at her. 'You would have done the same, I fancy. I've been high-handed, haven't I, but the matter is urgent. Authority doesn't like to be left hanging around.'

'No. I—I wouldn't have known what to do anyway.' She drank her coffee and some of the burden of sadness seemed to have been lifted from her shoulders. 'I still can't believe it.'

'That's natural, and it's nature's way of protecting you until you can cope again.' He finished his flan. 'Now go to bed, Clotilde, and go to sleep. I'll clear away these things. If you can't sleep, come and say so and I'll give you something. Where am I sleeping?'

He was as calm and matter-of-fact as a brother. 'The first door on the left at the head of the stairs.' Suddenly bed seemed a nice place to be; shock and grief had numbed her to a standstill and all she wanted to do was sleep. She said goodnight and went upstairs, and slept the moment her head touched the pillow.

Dr Thackery left soon after breakfast, but not before he had written a list of things to be done and which would keep her, and Rosie, for that matter, busy until his return. 'I'll phone you before we leave France,' he told her. 'Two or three days' time, I expect—if there's a delay, I'll let you know.' He went out to the car and Clotilde went with him, reluctant to see him go. 'I'm going to St Alma's first, and I'll be in touch with your solicitor.' He looked away from her, across the garden. 'Perhaps Johnson could manage to come down and be here when I get back?'

'I expect he'll ring.' Clotilde put out a hand and had it engulfed and held. 'I'll never be able to thank you enough. Oh, dear, I suppose I'll say that whenever I see you!'

He smiled. 'I daresay someone will do the same for me one day.'

She nodded. 'I quite forgot to ask you; about money—I mean, it must be costing a great deal, I can ...'

'I'll settle with your solicitor later.' He bent and kissed her cheek. 'Get Johnson down here as soon as he can manage it—someone can take over for him for a few days.'

He drove off with a casual wave, and she stood watching him go, suddenly engulfed in unhappiness again. But there was no use in standing there feeling sorry for herself: there was that list to work her way through, friends to write to, to telephone, the vicar to see, as well as the house to run. Rosie had been given a list too, and Clotilde went back to the house to find her and read it. Dr Thackery seemed to have thought of everything. 'We'd better tick things off as we see to them,' said Clotilde.

And so the next two days went by somehow. She ate and drank and slept and worked her way faithfully through her list. Soon after Dr Thackery had left she rang the hospital and asked for Bruce, but he wasn't available. 'But I'll get him to ring you as soon as he's free,' the sympathetic receptionist told her.

Which wasn't till the evening. Worth waiting for, Clotilde told herself, just to hear Bruce's voice asking how she was, telling her that he'd been up to his eyes all day. 'But I'll see you some time tomorrow,' he promised.

It was only when she had hung up that she realised that he hadn't asked her how she was managing. Perhaps he thought there was an uncle or cousin or old family friend. But tomorrow he would be with her, she told herself as she got ready for bed that evening. She needed him badly. She had no tears left, but there was a hard lump of misery in her chest which she had to conquer, and she didn't think she could manage it by herself.

Bruce didn't come. Rosie had cooked a proper meal that evening; they waited and waited, and it wasn't until almost ten o'clock that he phoned—an emergency which Sir Oswald had asked him to deal with, and Clotilde, keeping her temper with an effort, longing to scream and rail at him, asked: 'Aren't I an emergency?'

'Of course you are, darling, you must know how I long to be with you; but this poor chap . . . well, never mind that now. At least he's going to recover.'

Clotilde felt mean and petty and ill-used at the same time. She was fighting to keep her voice normal when the operator broke in to say that there was an urgent call from France, and would she take it. She hung up without saying goodbye to Bruce and a moment later Dr Thackery was on the line.

'You sound as though you're crying,' were his first words after she had mumbled a greeting. 'We'll be back tomorrow around tea time. I'll see you then.' And when she didn't answer: 'You don't want to talk, do you? Eat your supper and go to bed. Goodnight, Clotilde.'

She hardly slept that night, and nor, she suspected, had Rosie. They busied themselves around the house and Clotilde took Tinker for a long walk after their scratch lunch, leaving Rosie to have a rest and then make her preparations for a meal that evening. Dr Thackery and her father's solicitor would be tired and hungry when they arrived.

It was going on for four o'clock when Bruce arrived and Clotilde, just for a while, found comfort in his sympathy and concern. She had gone to the kitchen to help Rosie with tea when she heard the Bentley stop outside the door, but before she could get there, Bruce had gone out to meet the two men. As she reached the door she heard him talking to them, for all the world, she thought indignantly, as though he had been there all the time, arranging things and looking after her and Rosie. What was more, as she joined them he observed: 'I'm here to cope with everything now, I'm sure you'll be only too glad to let me take over.'

Dr Thackery wasn't looking at him, though, he was staring at Clotilde's bewildered angry face. He said: 'Hullo, Clotilde,' and when he saw the tears sparkling in her eyes: 'Everything's all right, don't worry.' And then to Bruce: 'I'm glad you managed to get here.' His voice was dry and Bruce gave him an uncertain look.

There was a little pause before Clotilde said: 'Well,

do come in, we've just got the tea ready, and Rosie's
been busy getting a meal prepared for you—we weren't
quite sure when you would get here.'

They all went into the sitting room and Dr Thackery
followed Clotilde to the kitchen. At the door he put a
hand on her arm. 'Just hang on for a bit longer,' he
urged her. 'After tea we'll have a talk, you and I and
that will be the worst part over.'

He opened the door, put a friendly arm around a
tearful Rosie and carried in the tea tray. He carried,
metaphorically speaking, Rosie in as well, ignoring
Bruce's raised eyebrows, and sustained a conversation,
not one word of which Clotilde could remember
afterwards.

And after tea he carried Clotilde off to her father's
study, with the mild observation that the solicitor and
Bruce could entertain each other for a short while, and
once there, he sat her down in one of the elderly
armchairs and gave her a sensible, down-to-earth
account of his journey. But his sympathy was real and
he dealt gently with her. All the same, she wept a little,
snivelling into his shoulder, and he made no effort to
stop her. At length she dried her eyes, mumbled that
she was sorry and sat up straight. 'What happens next?'
she asked.

He told her with a calm matter-of-factness which she
had learned to expect, for it was his way. 'You'll come
to the funeral?' she asked finally.

'Of course, if you would like me to. Have you any
family at all?'

She shook her head. 'My brother-in-law phoned—
Laura, my sister, hasn't been told. There isn't anyone
else, except friends, of course.'

He nodded. 'There are some things I brought back

with me. I'll take them upstairs to your parents' room, if I may—you can deal with those later.' He pulled her gently to her feet. 'Now we'd better go back, hadn't we? Is Johnson staying the night?'

'Oh, no. He's got a list in the morning, but I'm sure he'll come again.' The doctor didn't say anything, only opened the door and he ushered her out. Crossing the hall, he observed; 'Mr Trent will want to go home, I expect, and since Johnson is here, I'll not need to stay any longer.'

His words were a disappointment to her. There wasn't any more to be said, she knew that, but he was such a comfort to have around the house and he knew exactly what had to be done and did it with a quiet competence which he made no effort to advertise.

'You won't stay to supper?' she asked.

'No need, with Johnson to keep you company; you'll have all the evening together.'

Clotilde said 'Yes,' rather doubtfully and led the way back to the others.

Almost the whole village turned out for the funeral, although only a few people, about a dozen or so, went back to the house afterwards. Bruce had been there, of course, solicitous in his care of her, very much in charge, and she was grateful for that. Dr Thackery had been there too, a quiet figure in the background who had made his excuses once they reached the house again and gone off, brushing aside her thanks. 'Don't come back until you feel that you can cope—on the other hand, don't stay here and mope. Is there anyone to keep Rosie company while you're at St Alma's?'

Clotilde was grateful for his concern for her loyal friend. 'She's got a niece—I'm sure she'd come and stay for a little while.' She smiled at him. 'You think of everything, don't you?' She offered her hand. 'Thank you again, Dr Thackery. I'll be back on the ward quite soon—I—I'll need to fill my days.'

She watched him go with a pang of regret.

Mr Trent was waiting for her. 'My dear, if you can spare ten minutes—people are leaving already, I see. There is the will . . .'

Half an hour later Clotilde left Bruce sitting by the fire and went with Mr Trent into the study. He sat himself down at the desk and when she had taken a chair opposite him, started to talk. He took a long time to come to the point, and she wondered why. A small legacy for Rosie, that was to be expected, and the remainder for her sister and herself. 'Only it isn't quite as simple as that,' he observed cautiously. 'This will was made many years ago and since then there have been changes. Rosie's legacy is intact, I'm glad to say, but I'm afraid that the rest . . . Your father mortgaged this house up to the hilt, and unfortunately, your parents were only insured for the first week of their holiday. I have no idea why, but there it is. There is virtually no capital and of course there will be the foreclosure on the house.' He added with sympathy in his dry old voice: 'I'm afraid you are practically penniless, my dear.'

Clotilde sat and stared at him. The unexpectedness of it numbed her brain. 'But I can't be! Father said Bruce should have the money to buy a practice when we marry . . .'

'Yes, he told me that, and in order to avoid making a new will, he put almost every penny of his capital into an enterprise started by an acquaintance of his. I warned him at the time, but if it had succeeded, the profits would have been substantial, and your father gambled on that.'

'Oh, poor Father! There's no chance . . .?'

'None, my dear.'

'I don't know just how much it was, but Dr Thackery arranged everything—he must be paid, of course, even if I have to do it monthly out of my salary.'

Mr Trent coughed and shuffled the papers before him, remembering the conversations he had had with the doctor during their mission. 'There will be sufficient funds to meet all expenses,' he assured her blandly. 'There are a few debts of a trifling nature, household expenses, you know. When they are settled there will be a few hundreds for you and your sister. I'm very sorry, Clotilde, indeed I am. There is one thing—these things take time; you will be able to live here for some months yet.' He put his papers in his briefcase. 'I shall, of course, keep in touch with you and you have only to let me know if you need advice or help. Your father and mother were good friends of mine.'

Clotilde said in a tight voice; 'Yes, they had a great number of friends. They were happy here.' She didn't dare say more; the thought of leaving the old house almost choked her.

Mr Trent was in no hurry to go. He sat for a time, talking gently about nothing in particular, and she was surprised to see that he had been with her for an hour when he finally got up from his chair. She went with him to his car, thanked him for his kindness, assured him that she and Rosie would be all right, and stood on the step until he had driven sedately away.

She would have to tell Bruce. Her heart sank at the thought; it would be a bitter blow to him—to them both. Bruce had no family to offer to help and nor had she. It would mean that he would have to go as an assistant in a practice and she would have to go on

working, even if they married. Certainly it put paid to
Sir Oswald's offer. She lifted her head and walked
quickly into the sitting room. The quicker she told him,
the better.

The room was empty and after a moment she went
along to the kitchen; he might be there with Rosie. But
he wasn't. Rosie was sitting in her shabby old chair by
the Aga with Tinker at her feet.

'There you are, love. Dr Johnson waited as long as he
could. He said he simply had to get back to the
hospital.'

'But he didn't say . . .' Clotilde didn't finish what she
was going to say; there was no point in feeling hurt and
surprised. Bruce was a busy man, and his time was
seldom his own. 'Oh, well,' she said with forced
cheerfulness, 'we'll have that marvellous meal together,
Rosie. There are some things I have to tell you too.'

She told Rosie everything, and why not? She had
been with the family for so long that she was part of it.
At first she refused the annuity. 'Better you had it, Miss
Tilly—I've got my niece to go to and next year I'll have
the old age pension.'

'No, Rosie, Father and Mother wanted you to have
it—I've got quite a good salary, you know, and I live
at the hospital. There's one thing, Mr Trent says we
shan't have to go for several months, that'll give us time
to get things straightened out.'

'You'll be getting married, no doubt. Nothing to wait
for, is there?'

Clotilde hesitated. 'Well, Rosie, it's like this—Bruce
wants to buy himself into a practice. It was all
arranged, Father was going to give us the money when
we married, but of course, that's not possible now.'

'Maybe not, Miss Tilly, but Dr Johnson's got a good

steady job, hasn't he? And I suppose you could go on working until the babies come.'

'Yes, yes, I suppose so. We'll have to talk about it. I'll be seeing him soon, I expect. Did he say if he was going to phone?'

Rosie shook her head. 'Not a word. To tell you the truth, he was a mite put out because you were so long with Mr Trent. Said his time was valuable and he couldn't hang around for hours.'

A bit different, thought Clotilde, from the Bruce who had been the picture of efficient, caring concern in front of all those who had come to the funeral. She checked her thoughts with something of a shock; he had been kind and thoughtful and he was a busy man, it must have been difficult for him to have got away from St Alma's even for a few hours. She hated herself for being disloyal and promised herself she would ring him up presently and thank him for coming.

The next few days went by on dragging feet. There were a number of sad little jobs to do and when they were finished with she turned her attention to the garden. It was a charming place, her father's pride, and it needed tidying up for the winter, although there were still masses of late summer flowers. But there were leaves to sweep up, and the last of the roses to dead-head, and the chrysanthemums to tie back. And there was Tinker to take for walks; a subdued dog these days, and Clotilde was beginning to worry as to what would happen to him. Thank heaven, she thought for the hundredth time, that they had a respite of a few months in which to plan the future for the best.

She found herself wondering about Dr Thackery and wished she knew him well enough to tell him of the turn of events and ask his advice. But he had already done enough, she decided, and Bruce would surely advise her.

She had telephoned on the day after the funeral, but he hadn't been in the hospital and he hadn't phoned either. At the end of a week she wrote him a brief letter, saying that she intended returning to work in two days' time. She wrote to Sally, too, and the Senior Nursing Officer and Fiona Walters.

Bruce telephoned the next day. He had been rushed off his feet, he told her, but he would be down on the following afternoon to drive her back. There would be a lot to talk about, he added, they could discuss their future on the way.

Clotilde packed her few things, made sure that Rosie's niece would be coming, arranged for the teenage son of a neighbour to take Tinker for at least one walk a day, then sat down to think what she was going to say to Bruce. It was going to be difficult and she dreaded it.

He arrived after lunch and his greeting was all that she could have wished for; the faint feeling of disquiet she had been experiencing about him must have been a result of the awful happenings of the last week or so. She bade Rosie goodbye, begged her niece to make herself at home, give Tinker a final hug and got into the car.

They drove for a few minutes in silence until Bruce said: 'Well, it's been a rotten time for you, darling. But now you must look ahead. I've been thinking, as soon as the will's proved and the money free, I'll buy myself in and we can get married. Sir Oswald's willing to wait a month or two. It's more than your father was going to give us, but I thought perhaps you'd put some of your own money into it.' He gave a little laugh. 'You shall have it back a hundredfold when I'm famous!'

'There isn't any money,' said Clotilde dully. It wasn't the way she had intended to tell him, but there was no help for it.

'No money? Darling, if it wasn't such a serious matter, I'd believe you were joking!'

'I'm not. It's true, there is no money—even the house has to go. I was going to tell you when Mr Trent went, but you'd gone, and it's not the sort of thing one can shout down the telephone.'

'Your father promised . . .' persisted Bruce, and his voice had a peevish note.

'Yes, I know. I'll tell you exactly what Mr Trent said.' She gave him the account of the interview word for word, talking into a silence which got colder and colder.

'My whole future,' burst out Bruce, 'it's ruined! Where am I going to lay hands on money like that?'

Clotilde's head was beginning to ache. Bruce wasn't behaving in the least like she had hoped he would. She had known that he would be bitterly disappointed, but then so was she. He could have made the best of it, and reassured her; now he was behaving as if she were to blame.

'You could marry an heiress,' she suggested tartly. It frightened her a little when he didn't answer her.

He hardly spoke for the rest of the journey, but let her out at the hospital entrance, put her case inside the door, said briefly that he would see her later on, and drove off.

'He'll get over it,' she muttered as she went over to the Nurses' Home. 'It's the surprise after being so sure.' She went into her room and found that someone had put flowers in a vase on her dressing table and laid out her uniform ready for the morning, and before she had time to unlock her case, Fiona came in with tea, strong and dark and well sugared.

'Hullo, love,' she said cheerfully, 'we're all so glad to have you back. Your Staff's been out of her mind, says nothing on earth will ever induce her to take a Ward Sister's post!'

She refilled their mugs and went to sit down in the bed beside Clotilde.

'Look, if you don't want to talk about it, okay, but if you do, we'll all listen and help if we can—you know that, don't you? We kept our heads down because Bruce will have been with you. I heard him telling Dr Thackery that he was seeing you every day and helping you get things sorted out.'

Clotilde took a long breath. 'Oh? It was nice of Dr Thackery to enquire.'

Fiona gave her a puzzled look. 'Well, he sent all those messages via Bruce, you must have had them. I expect you've had so much to do you've forgotten.' She hesitated. 'We were wondering—when you have days off, if you'd like one of us to come with you, just for a bit, you know.'

Clotilde's hard-won calm broke, she gave a great sniff, too late to stop the tears. 'Oh, you are dears, all of you. I can't think of anything I'd like better. There's an awful tale to tell you, but if you don't mind I'll wait a bit.'

Fiona poured more tea. 'Drink up, love. You talk when you want to and not before, see? Now you're going to wash your face and powder your nose and we're taking you out to supper. Tomorrow's time enough to go to the dining room.'

Clotilde had half expected Bruce to give her a ring, even to arrange to see her, but there was no word. She went with her friends and ate the supper they ordered for her, then went to bed and, strangely, to sleep.

Breakfast was something of an ordeal, but once she had taken the plunge it wasn't too bad, and the ward, once she was back on it, hadn't changed all that much. A few new faces and no Mrs Perch, but Miss Knapp was still there, having had a few bad turns hours before she was due for discharge.

Clotilde sat in her office, reading the reports for the last week, listening to Sally and gradually gathering the reins together again.

'And it's Dr Thackery's round,' Sally reminded her.

'Good lord, I'd quite forgotten! Is there anything special I should know?'

She was brought up to date, given a cup of coffee and told not to worry. 'He's been an utter darling,' said Sally. 'I mean, all sorts of things went wrong because you weren't here, but he never said a word. Would you like me to come with you when you do your round?'

'Yes, please. Thank heaven we don't have such a quick turnover as the surgical side.'

'More coffee?' asked Sally, and then: 'I've not said anything, Sister, but we're all ever so sorry, only we thought you'd rather not talk about it just yet.'

'You're all very kind—and you're quite right, Sally, I don't want to talk about it for a bit. Coming back to work will help enormously.'

Clotilde did her round, picking up the threads easily enough so that when the ward doors opened and Dr Thackery and his team came through them, she was as calm and cool as she always was, only her pretty face was far too pale, and there were shadows under her eyes; very unhappy eyes.

He greeted her quietly, for all the world as though

they had never met other than on the ward. He made his unhurried way from bed to bed and finally went to her office as he always did, to have his coffee and talk over anything he saw fit to discuss. Dr Evans, as usual, hung on every word he uttered, looking adoringly into his face, something which he quite obviously didn't notice. He got up at length, nodding goodbye and strode off to Men's Medical, leaving Clotilde feeling vaguely hurt.

She tidied the papers on her desk and told herself briskly that she was being sorry for herself, and that was a waste of time. I'll feel better when I've seen Bruce again, she decided, the uncertainty of not knowing just how he felt was doing her no good at all. If only he would come!

The door opened and she looked up, thinking like a child that her wish had been granted. It was Dr Thackery.

'I'm glad to see you back,' he told her. 'What's the matter, Clotilde? Johnson told me you were fine, making plans for the future, that he was seeing you each day. What's wrong?'

She stared back at him, determined not to cry. He looked so kind and understanding and she had to talk to someone. After a moment she said stonily: 'Everything's gone wrong, but if I tell you now, I'll start to howl.'

He smiled faintly. 'In that case, we'll make a date, shall we? When are you off?'

'At five o'clock.'

'I'll be outside at half past five. Do you want to bring Johnson along too?'

'No, oh no—you see, it's partly to do with him.'

'Ah, just so!' There was a gleam, quickly hidden in his eyes. 'We'll talk later.'

CHAPTER THREE

SEVERAL times during the course of her busy day, Clotilde regretted her impulsive remarks to Dr Thackery. What a spineless creature he would think her, a great grown woman who had been holding down a job for some years, not even very young and inexperienced. Besides, wouldn't it be disloyal to Bruce to discuss their affairs with him? On the other hand, she needed advice badly and Mr Trent, although sympathetic, was too old. And it wasn't just for herself she neded help, there was Bruce to consider—his whole future might be at stake, and then there was Rosie, safe for the moment, but in two or three months' time she would have to find a home—and Tinker. She tried her best not to think about it as she went through her ordered day, serving dinners, the medicine round, the sudden emergency of old Mrs Brooks having what she called one of her spasms, and which was, in fact, a heart attack. Making out lists for clean linen, diets, off duty, smoothing out the hundred and one creases in the fabric of the ward's day. She went off duty feeling tired and dispirited and wishing very much that she could go to her room and stay there, undisturbed. But of course, she couldn't do that; Dr Thackery had been kind and helpful when she had needed both kindness and help desperately and she owed it to him to keep their date. She showered and changed into her grey flannel suit, applied make-up in a perfunctory fashion and went down to hospital entrance.

47

The Bentley was there. He got out when she came through the swing doors, remarked on her punctuality in a placid voice, installed her beside him and drove off.

'Somewhere quiet,' he observed, 'where we can talk in peace. Do you know Oxfordshire at all? There's a village called Roke—there's a good restaurant there— an inn really, it stays open until late, so we shan't need to keep an eye on the clock. Why not sit back and close your eyes? It must have been a hard day for you.' He gave her a brief sidelong glance. 'We know each other well enough not to have to keep a conversation going unless we want to.'

'It's such a comfy car. I'm glad to be back at work, though.'

He didn't answer, and presently she did as he had suggested and closed her eyes. When she opened them it was already dusk and they were in open country.

'Almost there,' he told her as she sat up. 'A little early for dinner, but we can sit round the fire and have a drink first.'

The inn was charming; warm and inviting and at that early hour, almost empty. The bar was small, dimly lighted, and the log fire burning in its wide brick hearth gave out a pleasant warmth. Dr Thackery ordered drinks, asked for the menu and suggested that they should dine in an hour's time, rambling on gently about nothing in particular while they chose what they should eat. Clotilde, who hadn't felt hungry, found herself taking an interest in the food after all, and presently when the waiter had gone and they sat alone with their drinks beside them, she discovered that she didn't feel tired any more. The nap in the car had revived her and her surroundings were exactly right; warm and comfortable and no bright lights to show up her puffy eyelids and white cheeks. She was discovering that there were degrees of unhappiness. One could be unhappy, but with the right person with one, some of the awfulness was taken away without a word being said. She looked across at her companion stretched out comfortably on the other side of the hearth and he smiled and said:

'Start away, Clotilde. And don't bother to get things in order, just get it off your chest.'

She took him at his word. It all came tumbling out, a muddle of words, half finished sentences, long pauses while she held back tears. 'So you see,' she finished, 'it's all the most frightful mess and I don't know what to do.'

And when she paused; 'You've talked to Johnson—but only yesterday, is that right? Why didn't you tell him when Mr Trent first told you?'

She hadn't meant to tell him that, but there was no point in holding back anything now. 'He had to go back to St Alma's, and—and then he was too busy to phone and he couldn't come down . . .'

'I see. Did you discuss your future at all while I was in France? You saw him frequently, I gather?' His voice was very bland as he asked the question.

'Well, no, he wasn't able to come and see me—not until the afternoon you and Mr Trent came back.'

Dr Thackery's heavy lids lowered themselves over his eyes. 'Ah—it had crossed my mind, and I must admit I found it curious that you hadn't replied to my messages after I returned. You see, I thought he was seeing you each day.'

'I'm sure he would have done, only he really couldn't get away.' Clotilde made the excuse eagerly. 'I'm not blaming him, really I'm not, but he's very disappointed and that makes it . . .' she paused. 'It's a bit ghastly coming on top of everything else.'

The doctor examined his fingernails. 'I agree with you. May I ask what sum was involved?' She told him and he nodded. 'A considerable amount. All the same, there are alternatives, you know. He is a young man and good at his work; he is tolerably well paid; there's no reason why he shouldn't stay on in his present job and marry you. Other men have done just that. Ambition is a fine thing, but sometimes we aim too high and lose our happiness.'

'But he wouldn't be happy. Don't you see? His whole aim is to become a consultant surgeon as quickly as possible.'

'That's still possible—not quite as quickly as he would like, perhaps, but after ten years or so, there's no reason why he shouldn't apply for a consultant's post and get it.'

'He wants a private practice . . .'

'Very nice as a sideline, but not essential. What would you like me to do? Talk to him? No, perhaps not, he doesn't like me overmuch. Talk to Sir Oswald?' He smiled a little. 'I don't think that would help very much; even a junior partnership would cost a lot of money.'

The waiter came back and he ordered more drinks even though Clotilde shook her head. 'I'm prescribing it,' he told her. 'And now we're going to talk about something else. You say the house is to be sold. What about the furniture?'

'I suppose I can keep that, only what would I do with it? I could give some to Rosie, if her niece will have her to live with her . . .'

'We must find somewhere close by—it would be cruel to uproot her after all these years—perhaps a cottage on a neighbouring estate where she could work for her rent? And that would be somewhere for you to go too. Would she be able to look after Tinker?'

'Well, I should think so. She might be glad to have his company and she'd have time to take him out.' She gave him a relieved smile. 'Why is it that you make everything seem so simple?'

'Because I'm not personally involved.' Just for a moment she thought he had sounded bitter, then she dismissed the idea as silly.

'What shall I do?' she asked him, and saw him smile a little, but not at her, she thought, at some hidden idea of his own.

'About Rosie, leave that for the time being—her future depends very much upon yours, doesn't it? Have a talk with Johnson. I would have thought that once he's got over his initial disappointment he'll want to make life as easy for you as possible, and the best way to do that is to marry you as soon as it can be be arranged, you might even go on working until you can find somewhere to live. Furnishing would be no problem, and once you were married you could put your heads together and see what can be done about Rosie and Tinker.'

She nodded slowly. 'You've been so very kind and understanding, and I'll take your advice. It's funny, we've worked together for several years now, and until last week I never really knew you as a person. I liked you, I always have—we get on well together, don't we—on the ward, I mean? I thought that was because we'd never got to know each other, I mean if you aren't personally involved with someone you're not likely to like or dislike them are you? Oh, dear, I've put that very badly!'

He was laughing at her. 'All the same, I get the gist of your argument. I gather we're friends.'

'Oh, yes—away from the ward, of course. I wish Mother and Father could have known you.'

He said very deliberately: 'Yes, tell me about them, Clotilde.'

And she did, astonished to find that she could at last talk about them with pleasure—sadness too, of course, but she hadn't realised until then how much she had wanted to. She felt the tension going out of her as he led her on to speak of her home and her childhood. When the waiter came to tell them their table was ready, she said rather shyly: 'I feel so much better, just talking about them, you know. I hope it hasn't bored you.'

'No, you had a happy childhood, didn't you?'

'Yes, very. A pity one had to grow up.'

'That has its compensations.' He smiled at her across the table. 'You'll enjoy giving your own children a happy childhood.'

The sherry had loosened her tongue, and now the claret they were drinking with their steak left it quite unbridled. 'Bruce doesn't think we should have children until he's established.'

'How old are you, Clotilde?' Dr Thackery asked.

'Twenty-five—well, to be quite truthful, I'm almost twenty-six.' She flushed a little under his thoughtful stare. 'Yes, I know, I'm getting on, aren't I?'

'No age—but Johnson may take ten years or more to get to where he wants to go.'

'And then it may be too late?' She sighed. 'I like children.'

'Ah, well,' he sounded cheerfully matter-of-fact, 'I expect you'll be able to make him change his mind.'

He began to talk about other things. They had their pudding and were drinking their coffee when he said: 'I shall be away for a week. Jeff will take over.'

Clotilde looked up at him with something like dismay. 'Oh—you won't be here . . .'

He said in his calm way: 'No, I shall be in Holland. My mother is a Dutchwoman and my grandparents are still living there. She married young, as did my mother. My father is a good deal older than she is.'

Three years, thought Clotilde, we've known each other, seen each other regularly, and this is the first time he's even given me a hint of his private life. She asked casually, hoping she didn't sound eager: 'Have you brothers and sisters?'

'Two of each, all younger than I,' and as she opened her mouth to speak and then shut it quickly: 'And I'm thirty-five. My name is James. I think it's about time you stopped calling me Dr Thackery, it makes me feel old.' He laughed suddenly. 'And no, I'm not married. I've not had the time.' He paused. 'That's not quite true, if I'd found the right girl I'd have found the time to marry her at the first opportunity, but I . . .' He paused and Clotilde finished for him.

'Never found the girl. But you will, I'm sure. Do you go to Holland often?'

'Oh yes, several times a year. My younger sister is married to a Dutchman and I've a number of friends there.'

He went on to talk about Holland, and their conversation stayed impersonal for the rest of the evening. Only as she was saying goodnight at the hospital entrance and she had thanked him did she wish him a pleasant holiday.

He thanked her gravely. 'And I hope to hear that the

banns are being read when I return,' he told her as he turned away.

It was ridiculous to miss him—after all, he didn't live in the hospital; he was there most days, but even if she had wanted to, there would have been no chance of talking to him. She saw him frequently enough, of course, in the ward twice a week, if there was an emergency and he had been called in; standing in some corridor talking to one or other of his colleagues. That was what she missed, she assured herself—his vast, reassuring form looming in the distance, or glimpsed going up or down a staircase. It was like losing a bit of familiar background.

She didn't see Bruce all the next day. It was after lunch, on her way back to the ward on the day following, that she bumped into him, going the other way. She stopped and smiled widely. 'Bruce—how nice! Have you been very busy? No one seemed to know where you were yesterday.'

He looked vaguely ill at ease, although he had taken her hand in his. He didn't answer her question but said with comforting eagerness: 'Are you off this evening? We'll go round to the local and have a drink.' He kissed her swiftly on her cheek and let go of her hand. 'I must fly. Make it eight o'clock.'

Clotilde went through her afternoon's work happily after that. Everything was going to be all right; there had been no hint of ill humour, no reproaches. Dr Thackery—James, she corrected herself, had been right; Bruce must have had second thoughts now that he had got over his disappointment.

It was busy on the ward. Sally had days off and there was a new student nurse to coax along, and over and above that, Dr Evans spent some time on the ward, getting in the way, demanding this and that, wanting to examine a patient just as teas were being served. Clotilde treated her with professional politeness, disliking her air of contempt towards both nurses and patients. She was a good doctor, she conceded, but her bedside manner was non-existent, and she put the nurses' backs up the moment she came on to the ward. She went, at last, and Clotilde settled down to write the outline report so that the part-time staff nurse who would be relieving her presently could fill in later. She was a nice girl, married and with two small children who were looked after by her husband while she was at the hospital. 'Not an ideal arrangement,' she had confided to Clotilde, 'but we do need the money, and Ned's a darling—never grumbles and is so patient.'

She came punctually, took the report, listened to what Clotilde had to say about the ill patients and then said quietly: 'I'm so sorry Sister—about your parents. It was a terrible thing. You must be so thankful you've got Mr Johnson. I expect you'll be getting married as soon as you can get things fixed up.'

Clotilde was at the door, ready to go. 'Yes—we're going out this evening to talk about it. He's been too busy to have time off . . .'

Her companion swept the look of surprise off her face before Clotilde noticed it. She had met one of the theatre staff nurses on the way to the ward, and that young lady had told her that Mr Johnson had had the whole of the previous day off and that morning as well. 'And very cock o' hoop he was when he came back,' she commented. 'Put us on the spot, too, with only our Freddy to operate.'

Freddy was a good natured, slow-moving young man, much liked by the nursing staff and tolerated in a friendly fashion by the other men. He cheerfully stood in for anyone wanting time off, never looked at the clock and performed operations with tremendous care and at a snail's pace. The two girls had speculated as to where Mr Johnson had been before parting. Somewhere Sister Collins didn't know anything about; making arrangements for their wedding perhaps, to take her by surprise. Watching Clotilde walking across the landing to the stairs, she did hope so.

The few hours Clotilde spent with Bruce were unmarred by any arguments—indeed, he avoided telling her anything about their future so assiduously that in the end she asked: 'Oughtn't we to make some plans, Bruce? I know it's early days yet, but perhaps if we explored a few possibilities . . .?'

He had flung an arm around her shoulders. 'Now just you leave everything to me, darling, you've had enough to worry you lately. Just relax and let things slide for a little while.'

She looked at him eagerly. 'Have you decided something? I know you can't have a practice, but you've got a good job at St Alma's and Sir Oswald thinks highly of you—he might be able to get you an even better post.'

Bruce laughed softly. 'Don't ask so many questions. Haven't I just said leave everything to me? When are you going to Wendens Ambo again?'

'I've got days off on Friday and Saturday. Could you come too?'

She didn't notice his hesitation. 'I'll see what I can do. Don't count on it, but I daresay I could manage something.'

Everything was all right again, she thought, getting ready for bed. Perhaps Bruce had his plans made and wanted to surprise her with them. She went to bed almost happy and slept better than she had done for some time.

She didn't see Bruce until Thursday evening, when he came along to the ward where she was writing the report. 'Up to my eyes,' he told her, 'but I'll drive you down tomorrow directly after breakfast.'

She beamed at him. 'Oh, good. Will you stay?'

'Can't say for certain until the morning, but I'll fetch you on Saturday evening—we might have a meal out.' He dropped a kiss on her cheek. 'Must fly. See you— usual place.'

Clotilde finished the report and stood for a moment before going into the ward for her goodnight round. Life was bearable again, only just, but at least she could think of her parents without bursting into tears, and look to the future. Grief was something you have to learn to live with, but the rest of life should go on normally. She closed the report book and went into the ward.

Bruce was already in his car when she got to the staff parking space the next morning. She got in, put her overnight bag on the back seat and turned to smile at him. 'A beastly day,' she said cheerfully, and indeed it was pouring with rain and chilly with it, 'but we can sit by the fire.'

He was already driving out of the forecourt. 'Sorry, darling, I'll have to come straight back—there's a perf for noon and Freddy isn't too keen on doing it. Everyone else is tied up—outpatients—so I said I'd help out.'

Her face fell, but only for a moment. 'Oh well, it can't be helped. Will you come down this evening?'

'I'll try—if not, tomorrow.'

'Well, at least we've got an hour or two now.' Clotilde settled back in her seat. 'Bruce, your appointment's up in a couple of week's time, isn't it? I forgot—there's been so much . . . Is Sir Oswald going to offer you another year?'

He didn't answer her directly. 'We'll have to wait and see.'

'Yes, but that's all very well. You must have time to look around for another appointment.'

He said shortly: 'Don't fuss, darling,' so that she fell silent. Perhaps she was fussing, she thought worriedly, but it was their future, something to be decided together and with care. Presently he did say: 'Sorry if I snapped; I've been busy—this drive is a godsend—just to get away.'

She cheered up at once. 'Poor you, I'm sorry. Let me know when you can get some days off and I'll fix mine to fit in—you can just sit around and do nothing. Rosie will love to have someone to cook for.'

'Sounds heavenly. A pity I can't stay for lunch.'

'Rosie will have coffee ready and she's sure to have made a cake.'

Rosie and Tinker gave them an enthusiastic welcome. The niece had gone to Saffron Walden to shop and spend the night with friends. 'She's a good girl,' said Rosie. 'It'd be lonely like on my own. We get on fine together.'

They had their coffee and cake round the sitting-room fire, and Bruce didn't linger. Clotilde went with him to the car and stuck her head through the window for a final kiss. 'I shall miss you,' she told him, 'but tomorrow's not far off.'

He didn't answer and she stood back, a little chilled because he seemed so absentminded.

'What's he worried about?' demanded Rosie when she went back indoors.

Clotilde didn't pretend not to understand her. 'Well, now that the practice has fallen through, we've got to make other plans,' she told her old friend.

'That shouldn't be too difficult. Get married, that's what.'

'Yes—well, I suppose we shall.' Clotilde didn't know she sounded hesitant and was surprised to hear Rosie's snort.

'A nice quiet little wedding here,' went on Rosie, 'with all your friends round you. Don't you go to a nasty old register office, your ma and pa wouldn't have liked it.'

Clotilde managed a smile. 'Of course not, Rosie. I'd like it to be here, just as they'd hoped.'

'Well now,' said Rosie briskly, and sniffed. 'I'm going to get lunch, and there's Tinker just asking for a good long walk.'

It was after lunch the next day when Bruce telephoned to say that he wouldn't be able to drive her back.

'But my car's at St Alma's,' protested Clotilde. 'I'll have to come by train.'

'I know—I'm so sorry, darling, but there's nothing I can do about it. You can get the village taxi to take you to the station, can't you? What time will you be back? I'll try and be around.'

'I'll catch the eight-fifteen; that makes it a bit late, but we could pop out for a drink if you like.'

'Fine, darling,' he sounded so pleased that she smiled at the phone. 'I'll give you a ring at the home.'

It was disappointing, but she was learning to be philosophical about it. She took Tinker for a walk, had

tea with Rosie and her niece who had just returned and
phoned for a taxi.

St Alma's seemed dark and grim in the damp
October evening. To live there and not be able to go to
Wendens Ambo each week would be ghastly. Clotilde
cheered herself up with the thought that once they were
married, they would at least have a home of their own,
however small. She began to think about mortgages as
she unpacked her bag. She had a little money saved and
there were the few hundreds Mr Trent had assured her
of, and surely Bruce would have something put by. He
wasn't an extravagant man and other than his car, his
expenses were few. It surprised her that she had never
wanted to know.

She went to supper presently, late but still in time for
the second meal that those who had been on duty could
have when they left the wards. And when she got back
to the home, there was a message for her to be in the
entrance hall. They were too late for a drink, but there
was a small café close by where they could get coffee.
Clotilde was so glad to see Bruce again that she hardly
noticed his preoccupied air, and when he suggested that
they went back to the hospital she agreed. He hadn't
said much about his day, but probably it had been a
busy one.

'How did the perf go?' she asked.

He didn't answer at once and then said: 'Oh, the
perf—very well—he's doing fine.'

He must be very tired, thought Clotilde with faint
worry; usually he liked to give her a blow-by-blow
account of his cases. 'You simply must get a couple of
days off,' she declared, and had to be content with his:
'Well, I will—do stop fussing!'

So they walked back to St Alma's, and although

Clotilde had her arm in his, she had never felt so far away from him. It would be better in a day or two, she told herself, getting ready for bed. He was overworked and worried and perhaps, like her, he felt frustrated at their not being able to see one another as often as they wanted to. She got into bed and lay for a while, thinking about it, and came to the conclusion that there was nothing much to be done about it at the moment. She would have liked to have talked about it to someone—James Thackery would do nicely, with his calm impartial manner and his certainty that things would sort themselves out. She was too impatient and she mustn't fuss.

She reminded herself of that several times during the next few days. She saw Bruce from time to time, but never for more than a few minutes, and it always happened to be in some place where all the world could see them. She wasn't sure whether she was pleased or vexed at the idea of seeing Dr Thackery again. The day of his return saw her on the ward in good time, making sure that everything was ready for his visit, and then, with time to spare, she went into her office to start on some of the paper work; there was a good half hour before he was due and he was always exactly on time.

But not this morning. She had picked up the laundry list preparatory to phoning the laundry and enquiring as to the dearth of pillowcases when the door opened and the doctor came in. His, 'Good morning, Sister,' was uttered in his usual casual friendly fashion, but his eyes searched her far too pale face. He closed the door and leaned against it. 'Problems solved?' he wanted to know.

Clotilde stared up at him, aware of the relief at just seeing him again. 'Well,' she began, 'you see, we never have time to talk, Bruce and I. He's busy or I'm on duty when he isn't, but he said I must be patient and not fuss, so I think he's doing something and isn't going to tell me until it's settled. I just hope Sir Oswald offers him another year's appointment—this one lapses in two weeks' time.'

Dr Thackery's face gave nothing away. He said kindly: 'Ah, yes, of course. Well, I'm sorry the banns haven't been read, but you've made some progress, haven't you? It isn't quite as hopeless as it seemed, is it?'

She agreed seriously and asked if he'd had a good holiday.

'Very pleasant. Terrible weather, though. Is there much new on the ward?'

She shook her head. 'Four new patients. Are you doing your round now? We're quite ready if you want to.'

He glanced at his watch. 'I've got someone to see first. I'll be here at the usual time.' He had gone as quickly and quietly as he had come.

Clotilde went back to her list and the telephone. He had been a little remote, she reflected, and found herself blushing. How boring for him having to listen to her moans; he had no reason to be interested; he had done his good deed and she must remember that and not impose on him further. She would be eternally grateful for his help and kindness when she had needed it so badly, but enough was enough. Next time he asked her about her plans, she would give him a bright and cheerful answer, even if it wasn't true.

She went to the ward door to meet him, as she had done so many times, wishing him good morning for the second time, and led him from bed to bed, the very epitome of professional competence and dignity, and studying his assured calmness, she found it hard to believe that this was the same man who had listened so patiently to her unhappy meanderings and actually suggested that she should call him James.

She caught his eye and realised that he had spoken to her, and he smiled very faintly as he repeated his suggestion that the woman he had been examining should have another blood count done. He turned to reassure his patient that it was merely a routine thing done at regular intervals. 'Just to make sure you're making progress,' he said kindly, and Clotilde, knowing that Mrs Duckworth was suffering from myeloid leukaemia and had a not very hopeful future, reflected, as she so often did when he was on the ward, that he was not only very good at his job, he was good at handling people too, passing on some of his own calm and never seeming to be in a hurry.

The round over, she led the way to her office for coffee. Dr Evans was there, of course, and Jeff Saunders, and the talk was all of the patients and their treatments. They got up to go presently, and she went down the ward and stood at the door while they filed through behind Dr Thackery, who after a brief 'Good morning, Sister,' was already striding towards Men's Surgical.

She had her days off the next day and since she hadn't seen Bruce she took herself off home, leaving a message at the lodge for him. Busy or not, he could at least have found time to say 'hullo'. Clotilde drove herself in the Mini, glad to get away for a while, glad too that it was a lovely morning, with a blue sky and a late autumn sunshine. She was looking forward to getting into the garden, and she and Rosie must put their heads together about housekeeping. Her mother had always had a well filled larder, but it would need replenishing; they could make out a list together and she would leave enough money to see Rosie through the next few weeks. There would be the rates to pay, and the gas and electricity and the telephone bill, she thought anxiously; she would have to see Mr Trent and discover just how much money there was.

But once back in her home, her worries receded. It was nice to be welcomed and made much of, to go upstairs to her own room and change into slacks and a sweater and go down to the kitchen for Rosie's excellent coffee and her gentle gossip about the village. That it would have to end soon was something she put out of her mind; just now she was content.

There was a phone call from Canada that afternoon to say that her sister had had a baby girl. She had been told of her parents' deaths, but there was no chance of her coming over to England for the time being. 'Next year, Tilly,' she promised. 'And how about you coming out here and paying us a long visit? I'm so sorry you've got all the worry of seeing to things, but you've got Bruce.'

Clotilde agreed that she had Bruce, 'And I've written to you. There's such a lot to explain. Mr Trent was going to write too; he's been waiting for you to have the baby.' They talked for a few minutes more, then hung up. It might be an idea to go to Canada later on if Bruce didn't want to get married just yet. She might get a temporary job and get some money saved. 'Oh, poor Bruce,' she said, throwing sticks for Tinker in the garden. 'There must be some sort of way—if only I had a rich aunt!'

She went into the house for tea, resolved to see Mr Trent and ask his advice.

But as it happened there was no need of that. She spent two happy days at home and then drove back after supper. She parked the Mini, and because there might be a message for her at the lodge, walked round to the hospital entrance. Bruce was crossing the hall as she went in and she called softly: 'Hi—I'm just back. Did you leave a note for me? I was coming to look.'

He came towards her reluctantly. 'I guessed you'd be back about now—a pity it's late, we could have talked . . .'

'I'm not tired; we could go to a café and have coffee.' Clotilde smiled at him. 'You've got news for me, haven't you? Can't I know now?'

'What, now, with everyone listening to every word?'

There wasn't a soul in sight and she said so, but Bruce laughed and bent to kiss her. 'There's no hurry,' he told her. 'When are you off tomorrow?'

'Five o'clock.'

'I'm off at six, with any luck. Be at the car about half past six and we'll have a meal somewhere.' He kissed her again and turned away. 'I must see a couple of patients,' he told her, and walked quickly away.

She spent quite a time in futile speculation before she slept that night, and it was hard to keep her mind on her work the next day. Five o'clock had never taken so long to come, but come it did, finally, and she made her way to have a sketchy tea and change. Last time they had gone out together Bruce had been annoyed because she hadn't been dressed up enough; she chose to wear the grey flannel suit with a navy silk blouse and navy shoes—an outfit which would pass muster if he intended to take her somewhere special. And it would be, she decided excitedly; Bruce had said he had news, and he had looked excited. It was a pity that he had been reluctant to tell her, but it would be all the more wonderful now.

She found matching gloves and handbag, gave her burnished topknot a final pat, and went down to where he kept his car. He was already there and greeted her with a quite unusual heartiness and her spirits soared, to be somewhat dashed by his: 'You've got yourself up—I was going to the pub for something in a basket and a pint.'

'Suits me, and I'm hardly dressed for the Ritz, am I?'

All the same, she was disappointed, though she wasn't going to say so, but she did murmur a question as Bruce drove past the Fleece and Thicket where they usually went. In fact he drove for five minutes or more and finally parked the car outside a small pub tucked away in a side street in the city.

'We've never been here before,' observed Clotilde as they went in. Bruce was on edge and she wondered why, but he was so attentive, ordering their drinks and asking what she would like to eat, that she forgot that while she listened to him giving an amusing account of his day. It was a few minutes after they had been brought their chicken in a basket that she begged: 'Now tell me this news, Bruce.'

'You won't like it—I've been hoping you'd guess . . .'

She gave him a puzzled look. 'What should I have guessed? Hasn't Sir Oswald offered you a new appointment? Well, you mustn't worry . . .'

'Oh, do listen—how you do carry on! Can't you see how impossible it is? For us to marry? To even stay engaged? How am I ever going to make my way if I've got you to provide for—we would never save a farthing—it would be years before I could apply for even a junior consultant's post. I want to go ahead now, can't you understand? While I'm young. I'm sorry, darling, I adore you, you know that, but my work is very important to me; I'm determined to reach the top at any price.' He added almost accusingly: 'You must understand. I've got the chance of a marvellous post . . .'

Clotilde hadn't said a word. She had gone very white and she had the feeling that she was going to faint, only, she reminded herself, great strapping girls like her never fainted. All the same, she had to do something. She picked up her bag and gloves, stood up, and walked away very fast. She heard his not too loud 'Clotilde!' behind her, but she didn't pause. He wouldn't come after her because he wouldn't want to make a scene in the crowded bar. She went out into the dark evening and started to walk. She walked a long way, not having the least idea where she was going, her head empty of all thought, which was perhaps just as well. She found herself on the Embankment finally and looked up at Big Ben to see the time. It was almost midnight. Half the night gone, she thought thankfully, and in the morning she would have her work to keep her occupied. She was almost at Whitehall Place when a police car pulled up beside her.

'Are you all right, love?' asked the driver. 'It's a bit late to be out on your own.' He got out of the car and gave her a closer look. 'Not feeling too good, are you? Hop in and we'll give you a lift home.'

Clotilde said in a polite wooden voice: 'That's very kind of you. I didn't realise I'd come so far. I'm a sister at St Alma's—I expect that's rather out of your way.'

He opened the door and ushered her in. 'Ten minutes. You oughtn't to be out on your own, Sister.' He repeated, 'Anything we can do?'

She managed to smile from a wooden face. 'No, there isn't, but thank you for asking. I'll be all right—I just had to—to get used to something.'

They dropped her off at the hospital gates by the ambulance entrance and she thanked them and wished them good night and then went in through the side door to the Accident room. The staff nurse on duty gave her a surprised look, but beyond a, 'Goodnight, Sister Collins,' she didn't say anything. Clotilde went through the back passages of the hospital and so to the Nurses' Home, climbed the stairs like an old, old woman and gained her room. She undressed quickly, got into her bed, and because she was so exhausted with emotion, slept at once, to wake a couple of hours later and stay awake, her tired brain going over and over the things that Bruce had said.

CHAPTER FOUR

CLOTILDE got up long before she needed to and went along to the pantry and made tea before spending a long time at the dressing table doing the best she could with her face. She hadn't cried; she wished she could have done so, and at least her eyes weren't puffy or her nose red, there were purple shadows under her eyes and no colour at all in her face—something which her companions at breakfast were too quick to notice.

'Got a cold coming on?' someone asked sympathetically, and when she said yes, she thought she had, they offered various remedies, not quite believing her. After all, it was only a few weeks since her parents had died so tragically. Her colleagues bunched round her as they walked to their wards, offering a wordless sympathy that warmed her cold heart.

Providentially, the ward was busy. Miss Knapp was back again, making life unbearable for everyone who came near her, and an elderly deaf and dumb woman had been admitted, and since she was too ill to bother with lip-reading or the notes written for her, Clotilde spent a great deal of time making her understand about the various treatments she was to have. If it hadn't been for several cheerful Cockney women, always ready for a joke, the ward would have been a gloomy one. As it was, there wasn't much time to dwell on that; the nurses bustled to and fro and Clotilde wrote up charts, attended to Dr Evans' wants, which were many, and worked her way steadily through the administration.

She went off duty at last, glad that the day's work
had kept her too busy to think about herself or Bruce,
and when someone suggested that she might like to go
to the cinema with some of her friends, she agreed,
outwardly cheerful. It would pass the evening, and
sitting alone moping wasn't going to make things easier
anyway.

She slept that night and found that by keeping herself
busier than she needed to she could get through the day
well enough, and it was getting easier with each day
too. She was aware that there was gossip about her and
Bruce, but no one really knew anything and she had no
intention of telling them. Perhaps later, when she could
talk about it rationally, she would tell Fiona.

It was Dr Thackery's round the next morning; she
did her face with extra care, studying it intently. It
didn't look too bad and if she used blusher on her
cheeks she would look perfectly normal. Nothing like a
little colour, she encouraged herself, and was disappointed to find that it didn't help at all, only made her
face whiter than it was. She rubbed it all off and went,
rather late, to breakfast.

There were still several ill patients on the ward and
Dr Thackery hadn't seen them yet, which meant
that the round would take longer than usual. A good
thing, as since he had to go to Men's Medical
afterwards, he might decide not to stay for coffee and
certainly there would be no time for a leisurely chat.
Clotilde met him at the door as she always did, wished
him an over-bright good morning and avoided his eye.

She had been right—the round took ages, not that it
made any difference to their coffee break. Dr Thackery
settled himself in the chair opposite her desk with the
air of a man who had all day in which to do nothing,

and although the talk was of all the patients and their treatment, she was annoyedly aware that he was watching her, and when he got up to go she jumped up with alacrity, eager to see the last of him, terrified that he might make some remark about Bruce and destroy her hard-held calm. But he didn't, merely thanked her as he always did, bade her good morning and walked off with his team.

She sat down again when they'd gone and heaved a sigh of relief. Sally was in the ward seeing that the nurses were getting the patients ready for their dinners, and although she had a pile of charts and notes to sort out, Clotilde allowed them to lie on the desk before her. She was filled with an overwhelming desire to talk to Dr Thackery, to tell him about the awful thing that had happened and be allowed to weep all over him and be comforted—the very last thing she would do. She pulled the first of the charts towards her and lifted her pen as the door opened and he walked in.

Her pale face flushed and then went paler still. She found her voice. 'Have you forgotten something, sir? Or did you want to see a patient again?'

He ignored this. 'What's the matter?' he asked, quite sharply for him. 'You look as though you've been trampled underfoot. Has Johnson been upsetting you?'

He was standing in front of her so that she was forced to look at him. She said with some truth: 'I've not been sleeping well, otherwise everything is fine.'

He stared at her. 'Is it? Your future settled?'

'Yes—yes, it is.' And that wasn't a lie, she consoled herself, only a bit misleading, and if only he would go before she poured it all out and he would be forced to stand there and listen to her self-pitying moans. 'It's nice to have it all decided,' she added.

His, 'Very nice,' was uttered so blandly that she gave him a sharp look. He was staring out of the window at the vista of chimneypots and didn't return her look, and presently he went away, his, 'Goodbye, Clotilde,' very placid.

Over lunch with Sir Oswald, however, his feelings were far from placid, although not for one moment did he allow his calm manner to reveal them.

'He's not a bad surgeon,' observed his companion, 'not bad at all; he should go far. Pity he has no money—still, I've done the best I can for him. Leeds Hospital is a good stepping off point for him.' He laughed cosily. 'The first rung up the ladder, shall we say?' He sipped his coffee. 'He was engaged, you know, to that pretty creature on Women's Medical—of course, you know her—he's taken her decision not to marry him like a man, I must say, although as I pointed out, he'll go farther faster without her!' He added: 'She's pretty enough to marry anyone she fancies.'

'Indeed yes,' agreed Dr Thackery.

It was two days before he saw Clotilde again; he had come on to the ward to examine a patient Dr Evans wasn't too happy about, and Clotilde, called from her office by one of the nurses, had sailed down the ward to meet him. Her manner was pleasant and professional, but her eyes were miserable and deeply shadowed. She had come face to face with Bruce in one of the corridors that morning and given him back his ring which she had been carrying with her in the hope of just such a meeting.

He had gone red and taken it without a word, and she stayed only to wish him good luck in his new job before continuing on her way to the Path. Lab. It had, somehow, made everything final; she supposed that right up to that moment, she had held the faint hope that Bruce would seek her out and tell her that he loved her so much that he was willing to forgo some of his ambitions.

Dr Thackery spent ten minutes or so with his patient, then left without a word other than fresh instructions for Clotilde to carry out. But halfway along the corridor he turned back just as she was going into the ward again.

He said vaguely: 'I may not be here for the round . . . When do you take your days off, Sister? I prefer you to be on duty.'

'The day after tomorrow, sir, and the day after that. Which day will you be coming?'

He frowned a little. 'I will let you know.'

He turned on his heel, and after a minute she went back into the ward.

She drove herself home at the end of the following day, and even though it was barely six o'clock as she left the hospital, the evening was rapidly darkening. It took her some time to get out of London, but it was only a little over an hour later when she stopped outside her home.

Rosie was waiting for her with a meal, half tea, half supper, and she sat down obediently to eat it, Tinker pressed to her side and Rosie staring at her from across the table.

'What's up, love?' she asked presently.

'Bruce has given me up,' said Clotilde, and was surprised to feel nothing much but tiredness. 'He's got a high-powered job in Leeds.' She added quickly: 'It's quite all right, I'm getting over it—I suppose in a way I was half expecting it.'

'You've not been sleeping,' accused Rosie. 'You go

this minute and sit down by the fire while I tidy away these things. You have a nice nap and I'll bring you a hot drink, then you'll go to bed.'

Clotilde got up and dropped a kiss on the elderly cheek. 'What a darling you are, Rosie! I feel marvellous now I'm home, and I do believe I could doze for a bit. I feel mean leaving you with the washing up, though.'

'Pooh,' said Rosie. 'You disappear and do as I say— you can wash up all you want to tomorrow.'

The sitting room was cosy in the firelight and Clotilde curled up in an easy chair drawn up to the hearth. It was very quiet in the room and she wished it could stay that way endlessly, with no future to worry about and no feelings to be hurt. She was lulled to sleep by its peace within a few minutes.

When she woke up Dr Thackery was sitting in the chair opposite her, reading a newspaper. He lowered it as she stirred and then she sat up, gaping at him. 'However did you get here?' she asked, and, 'How long . . .? What's the time?' and then: 'Is anything the matter at the hospital?'

He put the newspaper down. 'I came by car, and I've been here for just under an hour.' He glanced at his watch. 'It's almost nine o'clock, and there's nothing the matter at St Alma's.'

She shook her head to settle her wits. 'Oh—then why . . .? Would you like some coffee or supper or a drink?'

He ignored that. 'Why didn't you tell me, Clotilde?'

She studied his calm face. 'It was really impossible to lie to him; if he had raised his voice or shown annoyance or anger it might have been different—as it was, she heard herself say meekly: 'I thought I'd bored you enough with my troubles, you might have said:

"Oh, lord, here she is again whining away and wanting sympathy and expecting me to solve her worries." So I wasn't going to tell you.'

He said mildly: 'I get my share of hospital gossip, you know. I had Sir Oswald's version over lunch yesterday.' He asked with interest: 'Did you jilt Johnson, Clotilde?'

Her dark eyes flashed. 'No, I did not! He took me out for supper and told me that his work was more important than I was . . .' She gulped back the lump in her throat. 'I would have been a hindrance, you see,' she finished bitterly.

'So now what will you do?' The doctor's voice was placidly enquiring and not in the least demanding.

'I have no idea.' Clotilde jumped to her feet, overwhelmed with the desire to burst into tears, even scream a little to relieve her feelings. Dr Thackery got up too, and somehow without knowing how it happened, she found herself with his arms round her, sobbing her heart out.

It took all of five minutes for her to sniffle and snuffle her way to an end. When she finally lifted her head she said with watery dignity: 'I'm so sorry, I don't know why I had to do that—so silly. And I can't think why you put up with it.'

'That's what friends are for.' He took out a handkerchief and mopped her face in a matter-of-fact fashion. 'You're going to feel better from now on.'

She smiled up at him and gave a great sniff. 'Oh, you are nice,' she told him. 'A splendid friend—you're always here at the right moment.' She chuckled: 'Well, at the right moment for me, at any rate.'

'I aim to please. How about that coffee?'

'And something to eat? There's whisky in the dining

room.' She asked anxiously: 'You don't have to go again?'

'I hoped you would ask me to stay the night . . .'

'Oh, please do. Rosie will be so pleased; she's been lonely even with her niece here, and cooking for the two of them is no challenge to her. If you could stay until lunch tomorrow she'll be up in the clouds.'

'Thank you—if you want me to?'

'Well, of course, I do. I'll ask her to make some coffee and get you something to eat—would sandwiches do? We had supper when I got here, but I could make an omelette . . .?'

He shook his head. 'Coffee and sandwiches sound fine, thanks. May I put the car away while you are seeing to them?'

Suddenly everything was bearable again; Clotilde smiled with something like content. 'Yes, do—and you'll be in the room you had last time.'

He came back into the kitchen just as she had finished the sandwiches and sat down at the table.

'Rosie's making up your bed; she'll be down in a minute and the coffee's ready.'

The three of them sat there, drinking their coffee while the doctor made inroads into the sandwiches. They talked about her parents, and afterwards Clotilde realised he had deliberately led her on to doing that. Nothing more was said about Bruce, it wasn't until she woke the next morning that she remembered that she hadn't thought about him once.

They had their breakfast, the three of them, at the kitchen table, then the doctor washed up while Clotilde and Rosie made beds and Hoovered and then, leaving Rosie to prepare lunch, they took Tinker for a walk—a proper country walk along bridle paths and skirting the edges of fields. There had been a slight frost during the night and the ground was hard under their feet, but the sun shone and they walked at a good pace, not talking a great deal. They had turned for home before he asked: 'Have you seen Mr Trent lately? Are your affairs going well?'

'I haven't heard. I suppose he's paying off what Father owed and . . .' She paused and went on: 'He said he'd settle up with you, for—for the expenses. Did he?'

'That's been dealt with long since,' he assured her. 'And it's still early days for the mortgager to foreclose. You will continue to work at St Alma's?'

'Well, yes. What else can I do? It's quite well paid, you know. I'd like to go away—oh, a long way away and start again, but how can I? With Rosie to look after and everything to settle about the house and the furniture . . . I wish I could turn my back on it all and then come back and find everything arranged for me.' She sighed. 'I had no idea I was so fainthearted. And everyone's been so kind. I know there's been a lot of talk about Bruce and me, but only behind my back, once he's gone it will all be forgotten.'

'But not by you.' His voice was very gentle and quiet.

'No,' she agreed sadly. 'I wondered if later on, when things are sorted out, if I took a job miles away—you know, out of sight, out of mind—that sort of thing.'

'A holiday?' he suggested. 'To see if you would really like that?'

'Perhaps. Do you think it's a good idea?'

'Yes, I do. Because when you come back to St Alma's you'll know if you really want to leave and make a new life somewhere else.' He was looking straight ahead and she thought how stern his profile was. 'You might think seriously of that.'

'Yes—well, perhaps I will. I'm beginning to feel I can start again.'

'Splendid. How about taking Rosie into Saffron Walden after lunch, it will be a little outing for her—we might have tea somewhere?'

'That sounds lovely.' She added: 'I'm on in the morning early . . .'

'We'll go back after supper.'

She stopped to look up at him. 'Why did you come?' she asked.

He shrugged massive shoulders. 'I wanted to know the reason for you not telling me about you and Johnson.' He sounded so casual about it that she didn't ask any more questions but started to throw sticks for Tinker.

The afternoon's outing was highly satisfactory. Rosie, delighted to be whisked off without warning, was even more delighted when the doctor made her a present of a handbag she had admired, treated her to a splendid tea and bought her a pot plant she fancied. 'It's like having a birthday,' she breathed. 'I haven't had such a nice time since your ma and pa gave me that bit of fur for Christmas.'

It was as they drove back that Clotilde realised that talking about her mother and father was no longer the pain it had been; she grieved for them, but it was a grief that she could cope with. Now she must disentangle herself from Bruce.

They drove back to St Alma's that evening, quite late after one of Rosie's splendid suppers, and parted with the casualness of good friends at the entrance. Clotilde had no idea where James Thackery lived and she wasn't particularly curious about it. She went through the swing doors with a backward smiling glance and up to her room. She had thanked him nicely for his visit and tried to explain without much success, how much it had helped her, but he had waved aside her thanks in a negligent manner. She had hoped that he might say when they could meet again, but he made no mention of it. 'And quite right too,' she told herself, getting ready for bed. 'He must have quite a social life of his own, and heaven knows he's wasted enough time on me in the past few weeks.'

All the same, she felt disappointed when he did his usual round a few days later and made no attempt to speak to her other than to give her directions about various treatments. 'Back to square one,' she muttered, watching his enormous back disappearing down the corridor. Not that there was any reason for it to be otherwise, only his comforting bulk had stood between her and her worries, and now it wasn't there any more, she missed it. 'Time you stood on your two feet, by yourself, my girl,' she told her reflection.

The gossip had died down, of course. Bruce was still around, but she contrived to keep out of his way, and pride had helped her to show a calm face to the world of St Alma's. And if she cried about it, she did it when she was alone. Her world was shattered, but she had the good sense to know that in time she would pick up the pieces.

Thank heaven, the ward was busy. The annual influx of elderly ladies with chest complaints was already in full spate, and early November was proving to be cold and damp and windy, none of which contributed to the comfort of those same elderly ladies living in poky flats with not enough heating and with little inclination to cook good hot meals for themselves.

Clotilde put up extra beds, coped with a shortage of

nurses, and found the days long. It was a relief when Bruce left. He hadn't come near her since that awful evening at the pub, and when occasionally they had unavoidable meetings around the hospital, he had given her an accusing look as though the whole miserable business had been her fault.

But even when he had gone, she still thought of him, not so much of him, perhaps, but of the life she had been looking forward to. She told herself vigorously not to look back but to plan for the future, but that didn't stop her wakeful nights. She would never look plain, but the sparkle had gone out of her, and although she gossiped and laughed with her friends and went out and about, it was an effort to do so.

She went home on her days off, of course, and when Rosie wanted to know when they were to see that nice doctor again, Clotilde told her calmly that he had a busy life with his own friends to be with in his free time, and that although he was such a comfort to them when they had needed that, they mustn't presume on his good nature and kindness. After which long speech Rosie fell silent, clicking her knitting needles with speed and glancing now and then over her spectacles at Clotilde, sitting opposite her with a book.

Clotilde, aware of the glances, went on reading; she had read the same page several times already; she would like to know herself why James Thackery had somehow become Dr Thackery, the coolly friendly consultant who discussed his patients with her twice a week, bade her good morning at the ward door and that was that. Perhaps she expected too much; she had presumed on a friendship offered when it was needed but which had now served its purpose. She toyed with the idea of asking him if she had vexed him in any way, and decided against it; he would be too nice to say so, and if he snubbed her it would be rubbing salt into the raw wound Bruce had inflicted.

It was a week later when Mr Trent wrote to her, a letter as dry as his conversation, stating merely that the few hundred pounds salvaged from her father's estate had been deposited in her account at the bank, and that the mortgager had informed that he intended to foreclose at the end of the month. 'I suggest,' wrote Mr Trent, 'that you visit me at a time convenient to yourself so that we may discuss this matter.'

Clotilde went the very next morning, providentially free until one o'clock, and was ushered into Mr Trent's office at the top of a winding staircase in a cramped house behind St Paul's Cathedral. The old man settled her in a chair, asked for coffee to be sent in, and shuffled the papers on his desk.

'There are a few small matters to deal with,' he told her as they drank their Nescafé and proceeded to deal with them in his deliberate way. Then he took off his glasses, polished them, and put them back on again so that he could peer at her closely. 'What I am about to say may be a surprise to you, Clotilde, but to me it can only be an act of kindly providence, and I think should be accepted as such.'

He took off his glasses again and looked at them, then put them back on. 'I have received a communication from a firm of solicitors whose client has bought up the mortgage on your father's property and who intends to live there within a few months—I understand that he intends to marry—moreover, he has stated the wish to buy the furniture *in situ* at a price to be ascertained by the proper authority, with the proviso that any pieces you might wish to keep for yourself should be excluded. Now, my dear Clotilde, that is a very fair offer and I most strongly advise you to accept it. What is more, he requests a caretaker for the house until such a time as he should move into the property and I would be able to recommend Miss Hicks—Rosie, I believe you call her?—for that position, which will assure a roof over her head for a few months at least. I cannot do more than urge you most strongly to accept this offer.'

Clotilde had been goggling at him, her mouth slightly open. She shut it firmly now and asked: 'What's his name?' And then: 'Are you sure he's on the level?'

Mr Trent looked hurt. 'My dear Clotilde, the solicitors involved are known by me personally. I can assure you that they are on the level, and their client also.'

'How long will it take? I mean, when do I have to decide what bits and pieces I want to keep?'

'A valuer will visit the house at a date convenient to you, and in due course I will appraise you of his findings.'

'Well, I suppose any day will do. I only have to phone Rosie to ask her to be in . . .'

'You would prefer not to be there yourself?'

She nodded without speaking.

'Very well. Shall we say in three days' time? If you would let Miss Hicks know. And in due course I will let you know the result of his visit.'

'And you are sure Rosie will be allowed to stay until this man moves in?' asked Clotilde.

'Quite sure. Who knows he might offer her the post of housekeeper when he and his bride take up residence.'

She said with false cheerfulness: 'That would be marvellous for Rosie.'

'And you, Clotilde? You intend to remain at St Alma's?'

She said slowly: 'I'd love to get away—right away, but I suppose I'm a bit scared—you know, finding another job, making new friends, finding somewhere to live . . .' She smiled at him. 'You've been very kind, Mr Trent, seeing to everything for me—it must have been very inconvenient for you, going to France unexpectedly.'

He said gravely: 'I'm your family solicitor, Clotilde. Do you see anything of Dr Thackery? It seemed to me that he was a true friend when you needed one badly.'

'He was very kind. I can't thank him enough.' She heard her voice, rather stiff and cool. 'But of course I don't see him much now—when he comes to the ward, twice a week, to do his round, you know. But he has his own circle of friends—it was just that he offered to help because he saw that I needed it. He would do the same for anyone—he's a very kind man.'

Mr Trent coughed. 'And Mr Johnson?' he asked quite guilelessly.

Clotilde had been expecting that. 'We aren't going to be married,' she said quietly. 'He's gone to Leeds, to another post—a better one.'

Mr Trent coughed again. 'I'm sorry, my dear, but there is an old saying concerning the shutting of one door allowing for another to open.'

He shuffled his papers and she took the hint. 'If there's nothing else I'll go, Mr Trent. And thank you once again.'

They shook hands and she was ushered out into the street, to walk back to St Alma's along the crowded pavements.

She reached the hospital entrance at the same time as the Bentley, and made to pass it, smilng briefly at Dr Thackery, but he was too quick for her; she had reached the doors when he caught up with her.

'The very person I want to see! Are you free tomorrow evening? My younger sister is here on a visit and I wondered if you'd be so kind as to have dinner with us. She's a good deal younger than I—just twenty-one—and she regards me as a bit of an old fogey. She's dying to go shopping too, and perhaps you could suggest where she could go for the kind of clothes she wears—rather way out they are too!'

He had been kind to her when she had needed kindness, so the least she could do was to accept. She did so in her normal calm manner and they parted to go their separate ways. It wasn't until she was in her room, getting into uniform, that she admitted to herself that she was excited at the idea of seeing him again. It would be interesting to meet him away from the hospital. She couldn't count the times she had spent with him at her home; they were hardly sociable occasions, and it might be fun to meet his sister. Perhaps she would find out something about his private life; it would give her something to think about and she was desperate to keep her thoughts busy. That way made it easier to forget Bruce.

Dr Thackery had his round the following morning. He greeted her in his usual placid manner, discussed his patients at some length, listened courteously to Dr Evans' theories, drank his coffee and took his leave and all without a word as to what time and where she was to meet him that evening. Of course, she reminded herself, he wouldn't do it while Dr Evans was there, but all the same he could have telephoned. She brooded about it, sitting at her desk, and when the phone rang, answered it, still brooding.

'Seven o'clock at the front entrance,' said James in her ear. 'Katrina insists on dressing up and going somewhere where she can dance—you won't mind?'

'No, I'm looking forward to meeting her. I'll be there at seven o'clock.'

'Good. I'll look forward to that.'

Clotilde spent a good part of her lunch hour combing through her dresses. Dressing up meant a long skirt, she supposed, and she spent some time wavering between a silver-grey jersey with a sequin strewn jacket, or a patterned organza in shades of pink. She finally settled for the grey; it was well cut and simple and in excellent taste, and besides, she had no wish to outshine James's sister.

As luck would have it she came off duty late. Dr Evans had come on to the ward during the medicine round and held everything up, wanting this and that and the other thing. Clotilde had held on to her patience with some difficulty, and when at last she went, repaired to her office to give Sally the report and fly over to the home. A good thing she had decided what to wear, she thought as she showered and dressed and did her hair with minutes to spare. She caught up the soft mohair wrap and her purse and tore downstairs, to slow to a dignified walk as she neared the entrance, quite forgetful that she was breathing very fast still.

The doctor got out of the car as she went through the door. He looked elegant in his dinner jacket, there was no denying it, and Clotilde was glad she had decided on the grey dress.

She smiled and said hullo a little shyly.

'You've been running,' he observed. 'Late off duty, I

suppose, and it wouldn't do to race out to meet me as though you couldn't get there fast enough, would it?' He chuckled. 'What did you do? Gallop as far as the back of the entrance hall and then sail to the door as though you had all the evening to spare?'

She laughed. 'Something like that. But I do like to be punctual.'

He got in beside her and switched on. 'Oh, dear—and I thought it was because you wanted to see me.' He spoke lightly and she answered just as lightly:

'But of course I did, and I'm looking forward to meeting your sister.'

They drove straight to the Savoy and found his sister and a young man waiting for them in the bar. 'Katrina,' introduced the doctor, 'and a family friend who's over here from Holland, Jan van Hegelstra.' He waited until Clotilde had sat down beside the girl, then he ordered drinks and sat down opposite them and started to talk to Jan. It gave Clotilde time to study Katrina and she liked what she saw—a very pretty girl, almost as tall as Clotilde herself, with fair hair and bright blue eyes, and she was glad all over again about the grey dress, because Katrina was wearing a bright blue crepe which would have clashed dreadfully with the pink. She sensed with pleasure that they were going to like each other and plunged into conversation. The talk soon became general, though, and presently they went into the restaurant. Clotilde had been once or twice before, but its grandeur struck her afresh. It was a place Bruce had never approved of—too expensive, he had always said, a waste of money when he could take her somewhere else and eat the same food for a third of the price. Not the same food at all, mused Clotilde, deciding between a delicious mousse and rillettes and having decided, weighing the merits of vol-au-vent financière against tournedos sauté Masséna, and having eaten these with a better appetite than she had had for weeks, accepting sherry trifle at the doctor's suggestion.

They danced presently. She partnered Jan first and then the doctor. As they circled round the floor he looked down at her, studying her face. 'You don't have to feel guilty,' he said softly. 'Life goes on, you know, your parents would want you to be happy again.'

'How did you know . . .?' she stammered a little. 'I'm not being a drip, am I? I'd hate to spoil Katrina's evening.'

'Don't worry, you're a valuable asset to our little party. Have you thought any more about leaving St Alma's?'

'Yes, only I'm being cowardly about it, I suppose. Besides, Mr Trent . . .' She stopped and coloured faintly, and when he prompted her gently: 'It's nothing, really.'

He didn't answer but when they reached their table again he led her to it, sat her down, glanced round to see the other two on the dance floor and took the chair opposite hers. 'Well?' he asked in a voice which expected an answer.

'I never meant to tell you—I—I seem to pour out all my problems to you, though this isn't really the place. It's just that someone's taken up the mortgage on the house. He doesn't want to live there yet, Mr Trent said, he's going to get married. He wants to buy the furniture, and Rosie may stay as housekeeper until he goes there to live.'

'That's surely good news?' James's voice was casually interested.

'Oh, yes. But it still only puts off the final bit, doesn't

it? I mean, sooner or later I must do something about it—I can't hang around waiting for something to happen.'

'No, of course not.' He sounded at his most placid. 'But neither do you need to rush into something without thinking about it first. Let things lie for a week or so. Shall we dance again?'

She agreed brightly, feeling a little hurt and let down because his interest was so casual even though his advice was sound. She would wait for a few weeks, as he suggested, and then make up her mind where she would go. Perhaps out of England for a time; she would be able to do that if Rosie were settled as a housekeeper.

'Stop thinking about it,' said James softly to the top of her head.

They stopped dancing presently and sat talking, and when Katrina asked Clotilde if she would go shopping with her if she had any spare time, she agreed readily. She had days off very shortly; she would drive herself home and spend the day, then return to spend the morning shopping with Katrina, who, if one were to believe her, hadn't a rag to her back.

It was midnight before the party broke up, Katrina and Jan to return to wherever they were staying; Clotilde supposed with James—and she to be driven back to St Alma's. As they went she asked diffidently: 'Do you live in London?'

His laconic, 'most of the time,' did nothing to assuage her curiosity.

He got out of the car at the hospital and went in with her. The entrance hall was quiet; the porter in his little office reading a paper glanced up at them and then went back to his reading.

'It was a lovely evening,' said Clotilde, and held out a hand. 'Thank you very much, James.'

'Delightful, and you look very pretty in that dress, Tilly. Next time we meet you'll be all starch and navy blue with that ridiculous cap on your head, and I shall have to call you Sister.'

'Well, that's what I am,' she observed matter-of-factly.

'You're a great many other things too,' he told her blandly, and bent and kissed her cheek lightly. 'Goodnight.'

She was left wondering what he meant and rather put out in case the porter had been watching them. There was no harm in a social kiss, but the hospital grapevine was capable of making a huge fire out of a little smoke!

CHAPTER FIVE

ROSIE was delighted with Clotilde's news when she got home, at first not believing her and then talking nineteen to the dozen about a rosy future for them both. 'I knew things would be all right,' she declared happily. 'You mark my words, Miss Tilly, everything's going to be just fine!'

A wish Clotilde heartily endorsed.

She went back to St Alma's that evening and set out for Harrods at nine o'clock the next morning. She was to meet Katrina there, something which she found frustrating, because she had hoped she would see James's home at last, but it seemed to her that he intended to keep his private life very much to himself and that she was to have no share in it, despite his friendly manner. Not that it mattered in the very least, she told herself robustly, waiting in the bus queue, for she had every intention of leaving St Alma's once the matter of the house and Rosie had been satisfactorily settled. A new life, she decided, jumping on to the bus at last, to be squashed between a stout lady in a cloth cap and a mild little man with a drooping moustache, somewhere exciting and sunny and warm—not too warm, of course; she'd have to work, not lie about sunbathing all day. Her vivid imagination had conjured up quite an interesting life for herself by the time she got off the bus, and it was rather a comedown to find herself on the damp pavement, a light drizzle misting her hair and tweed suit. She made for the nearest

entrance and got there just as Katrina got out of a taxi
and caught her by the arm. 'Let's have coffee first,' she
begged, 'and you can tell me where to go when we've
looked round here.'

Clotilde smiled. Katrina seemed years younger than
herself; she guessed she was the darling of the family,
accustomed to having her own way. 'Well, it depends
on what you want to buy,' she began.

'Everything,' said Katrina simply.

So Clotilde ticked off the best shops to go to if
Katrina didn't find all she wanted in Harrods.
'Although I should think they've got just about all you
want. Anyway, let's start with the separates, shall we,
and you should find some pretty dresses—long or
short?'

They decided this important question while they
finished their coffee and then began to shop in earnest.
Clotilde was secretly astonished at the amount of
money Katrina was spending. The separates were
quickly dealt with, the more serious business of
choosing clothes for the evening took up an hour or so,
and even then Katrina was by no means satisfied.

'You must go out a great deal,' observed Clotilde
when Katrina added a crêpe trouser suit and a satin
sheath to their ever-growing packages.

'Quite a bit. Now I want something really grand—the
Burgermeester's reception, you know, all white ties and
old ladies in satin . . .'

'I'm sure it's not as bad as that or you wouldn't
bother to buy something grand.'

Katrina laughed. 'You're right, of course. Where
shall I go for such a dress?'

'Well,' said Clotilde doubtfully, 'it's according to how
much you want to pay . . .'

Katrina looked taken aback. 'I pay? James said I could choose whatever I liked. I still have a lot of money to spend. See, he's signed these cheques and I fill them in.'

'My goodness,' said Clotilde, 'and you've spent a lot already.'

'I'm his favourite sister, and when I marry he'll no longer be able to buy me things, that will be for my husband.'

'Who'll need to be a millionaire,' Clotilde laughed. 'You really are the limit, Katrina! There's rather a nice boutique nearby—I bought a dress there when my sister got married.'

An hour later they stood on the pavement. Katrina had her dress, a blue crêpe that matched her eyes, yards and yards of skirt and a tucked bodice with shoestring straps, exactly right for the Burgermeester, she had decided, and handed over another of her brother's cheques.

'And that, I think, is everything,' she observed. 'Now we'll take a taxi and go home to lunch.' She turned a beaming face towards Clotilde. 'You will come, won't you, Tilly?'

'Well, I hadn't expected to——' she hesitated. 'You asked me to go shopping.'

'But we've had a busy morning and now we must eat. Please come; after lunch you'll stay a little while, and I'll try everything on and you can say if it's suitable.'

Katrina had a way with her; her eyes, as blue as her brother's beseeched her.

Clotilde got into the taxi Katrina had summoned. They were both laden with parcels, although several of the larger boxes were to be delivered. She longed to know where they were going and was still trying out several ways of finding out in her head, when the taxi stopped. They were in South Audley Street waiting for the traffic lights to change, but very swiftly, before she could frame her question, Katrina said: 'It's the next turning; James lives in a mews cottage.'

Somehow not in the least what Clotilde had imagined. True, she had never thought about it much, but when she had, the doctor had gone home to a vague modern flat with beige furniture and a daily house-keeper. But when she got out of the taxi she saw how mistaken she had been. The cottage wasn't really a cottage but a miniature Georgian town house, squashed in a corner of the mews, and with all the right trimmings; geraniums, still flowering on the windowsills despite the autumn chill; a solid black-painted door with a handsome brass knocker, shutters at the windows and a pristine white doorstep. She followed Katrina in as she unlocked the door and wordlessly handed over her parcels to a motherly soul who put her in mind of Rosie.

'This is Mrs Brice,' said Katrina, 'she does for James.' She flung an arm around her. 'She's done for him for a long time now, he'd die without her.' She added: 'And this is Miss Clotilde Collins, my friend.'

Mrs Brice looked pleased, clucked comfortably, said, 'Go along with you, Miss Katrina,' and then: 'Pleased to meet you, I'm sure, miss. Will you have lunch right away or wait a while?'

'We'll have a drink first, I think, but we'll make ourselves tidy first.'

The hall was square with a small staircase at one side. Its walls were panelled and it was thickly carpeted in a dark red which gave it a cosy glow. Clotilde, going upstairs after Katrina, looked around her with approval. Once inside, with the door shut, it was hard to imagine that one was in the heart of a big city.

The landing was carpeted too and had several doors leading from it as well as a narrow passage at the back. Katrina opened one of the doors.

'This is my room when I come to visit James,' she said, 'and that's not so often now. Mother and Father live in Dorset, you know, but I'm at Leyden University and live with my grandparents during term time. I like it very much, but I find it difficult to speak English when I've spoken nothing but Dutch for weeks on end. James, he had no difficulty, he's happy speaking both. Of course, we speak Dutch with my mother when we're at home, although we're English. You like my room?'

'It's charming,' declared Clotilde, and meant it. It was by no means large, but the bed and dressing table and tall chest were of yew and delicately made, and since the carpet and curtains and chair covers were in pastels the effect was of space and light. The windows overlooked a tiny garden, the merest plot, exquisitely tidy and full of greenery. It had a bird bath in its centre with a ginger cat sitting on its rim.

'There's a cat in your garden,' said Clotilde.

'Harry—he belongs to James. He's got a dog too, George—he goes with him sometimes when he has to drive out of town with Millie.'

So James was away. Clotilde, washing her hands in the little gem of a bathroom, felt regret.

They had their drinks in a surprisingly large sitting room, comfortably furnished with chintz-covered chairs drawn up to a small fire in the steel grate, several small mahogany lamp tables and a glass-fronted wall cupboard housing a collection of Delft blue. Harry had come in and curled himself up before the fire, and

Katrina flopped down beside him, leaving Clotilde to settle herself in one of the chairs. They sipped their drinks in a friendly silence until Katrina said: 'They promised to send the things from Harrods straight away . . .'

Clotilde glanced at her watch. 'There's hardly been time,' she observed mildly, then lifted her head. 'There's a car now—I daresay that'll be the van.'

She had her back to the window and she wouldn't have seen much, anyway; it was covered by a fine net curtaining and draped with chintz curtains drawn back with cords. There were muffled sounds from the hall, but the door was thick, it wasn't until it was opened and James walked in that Clotilde saw who it was.

He said placidly: 'Hullo—have I kept you waiting? I got held up on the way back.' He helped himself to a drink and sat down in a great wing-backed chair opposite Clotilde. He looked across at her and smiled.

'Have you had an exhausting morning? Kitty's a holy terror to go shopping with.'

'It was fun,' and Clotilde, saying it, realised that it had been fun; just for a little while she had been free of sadness and worries, and Katrina was a delightful companion. 'I enjoyed it.'

'Good. I suppose the house is stuffed with your parcels, Kitty?'

'I had a good morning and bought everything I wanted,' replied his sister happily. 'I'll go home tomorrow and pack my lovely new clothes and wear them in Leyden, and everyone will say how smart I look.' She grinned disarmingly. 'And you will miss me, dear James?'

His firm mouth quivered. 'Oh, yes, indeed I shall. It will be so quiet.' He turned his head as the door opened as large Great Dane lumbered in, acknowledged Clotilde's friendly hand on his head with a wag of his tail and then flopped down at the doctor's feet.

'He's tired,' declared Katrina. 'He must have been up early—what time did you leave, James?'

'Just before seven o'clock.'

'All that way,' observed his sister 'just to prod someone in the stomach and give a weighty opinion that it's indigestion!'

'How right,' agreed the doctor amiably, 'only unfortunately it wasn't indigestion.' He glanced at his watch. 'If lunch is ready, could we start? I'm due at St Alma's in just under the hour.'

And at the end of that meal, as he got up to go, he said casually: 'I'll be home for dinner—stay and dine with us, Clotilde, I'll drive you back to St Alma's afterwards.'

He paused at the door just long enough for her to say yes. Just as though she were an old family friend, a frequenter of his home, someone who knew all about him—and she knew next to nothing. Was this delightful house his, she wondered, or rented, fully furnished, for as long as he needed it, and where in Dorset did his parents live, and what exactly did Katrina do at Leyden? She could at least find that out.

'Me?' queried Katrina, looking surprised. 'Oh, don't you know? I'm studying Economics.' She giggled. 'James says it's very appropriate because I'm extravagant! But I do love clothes, don't you? Let's go up to my room and have a look at what I've bought.'

The two of them spent a pleasant afternoon. Clotilde curled up on the bed while Katrina tried on one thing after the other, then later they went downstairs again and had tea round the fire and talked again until the doctor's measured footfall, and his voice saying something to Mrs Brice, disturbed them. A moment later he put his head round the door.

'Pour me a drink, Kitty, will you? I'll be down in ten minutes.'

He looked tired, Clotilde thought, when he joined them, but immaculate. She had never seen him otherwise, and he was his usual placid self, wanting to know how they had spent their afternoon and when she asked him if he had been busy, answering her with a casual 'So-so,' which made her feel she shouldn't have asked. She coloured a little and looked up to find him watching her, and said the first thing to enter her head.

'This is a charming house.' Her voice came out rather high and too fast and he smiled faintly.

'I was lucky to find it, it's nicely in the centre of things without being noisy. I go down to Dorset whenever I can spare the time. My home is just outside Shaftesbury—Ashmore, a very small village indeed, but a delightful one.'

'Tilly must come and stay next time I'm home,' declared Katrina. She sat up straight looking pleased. 'Better still, I've got a super idea—James, you're coming to fetch me for the Christmas holiday, aren't you? Can't you bring Tilly with you? I want her to see Leyden.'

She looked at her brother; his blue eyes were looking very intently into hers and after a moment he smiled slowly. 'What a very good idea—that is if Clotilde would like to come . . .?'

They both turned to look at her and he said: 'Could you get three or four days off?' and then in a resigned voice: 'I do beg of you to agree, Clotilde, or Kitty will pester me for ever—she's utterly spoilt, you know.'

'Do say you will!' Kitty turned her imploring gaze on Clotilde. 'I promise you you won't be bored. James can go off with some of his dreary old professor friends and I can show you Leyden.'

Clotilde was aware of a vague wish that James might ditch his learned friends and show her the town as well. 'It sounds great fun,' she said carefully. 'Could I let you know? Off duty you understand, and if the ward's busy . . .'

'A sensible suggestion,' declared the doctor smoothly, so that for one moment she wondered if he was going to squash the whole idea after all. 'Although I did suggest to you that if you were to go away for a few days it might help you to make up your mind about changing jobs; there are vacancies for trained nurses in Holland, you know.' He put down his glass and sat pulling at George's silky ears, looking at her.

'Well, it would be very nice . . .'

'That's settled, then. I'll let you know the dates next time I see you, Clotilde.'

She wasn't given the chance to think it over or have doubts or even be a little annoyed at his high-handed assurance that she would agree to his suggestion. They went into the dining room, oak-panelled and not too large, with its oval mahogany table and Sheraton sideboard, thick velvet curtains shutting out the chilly evening, and the talk skimmed lightly over unimportant topics which firmly shut out serious conversation.

They went back to the sitting room for their coffee and sat, still talking idly, until Clotilde looked at the bracket clock in a niche in the wall.

'It's almost eleven o'clock!' she exclaimed. 'My goodness, I've been here hours too long—I'm so sorry, you must be wishing me to Jericho.' She looked at the doctor. 'And you've had a long day too.'

'But the last few hours of it very pleasantly spent.'

'What a shame that I have to go back,' began Katrina. 'James dear, could you possibly . . .?'

'No, child, I couldn't, nor would I if I could. You only have another two terms, and you know how pleased Mother will be if you get a degree.'

'Oh, well, yes, I suppose so. But you will come to Holland, won't you, Tilly, promise?'

Clotilde nodded. 'Yes, I'd love to see you again, and it's been a lovely day.'

In the car presently she said: 'Katrina's a dear girl, isn't she? I expect she's clever too?'

'Not very—just bright enough to scrape through her exams. Thank you for keeping her company today.' James swung the Bentley through the hospital entrance and got out to open her door, but when she would have wished him goodnight he went with her into the hospital. 'I've a patient to see—one of yours, admitted last night, and don't think I'm going to give you her diagnosis here and now, because I'm not, but I promised Mary Evans that I'd come in again and take a look . . . she'll be waiting for me.'

So it was Mary Evans, was it? Well, the wretched girl had been trying hard enough to catch his eye, thought Clotilde waspishly. She thanked him for her lift, wished him goodnight in the cool voice she used when showing consultants off her ward, and left him. She was halfway to the Home when she found herself wishing she had been rather warmer in her manner. After all, what business of hers was it if he was on friendly terms with his house doctor? Indeed, she told herself with undue briskness, she should be glad. What was more, she

would try and like Dr Evans; she wasn't unattractive in
a dim sort of way, if only she didn't gape at him in such
a silly fashion. Though perhaps he rather liked that; to
have someone gazing at one with adoring eyes and
listening to every single word one said. For the first
time in weeks Clotilde didn't give Bruce a thought, and
although she did think of her mother and father it was
with a gentle sadness which held no pain.

Of course, the next morning, all her problems came
crowding back into her head. True, for the moment at
least they were solved, but not her own future. James
had said let things ride for a bit and she didn't think she
would be able to do that. Before Christmas she must
make up her mind and then stick to it. She ate her
breakfast hurriedly and went on to the ward, to find it
even busier than when she had left it two days ago.
They had the same hard core of elderly chest and heart
cases who were still in their beds, of course, but there
were several new ones in various stages of illness, as
well as several patients who had relapsed unexpectedly.
The morning went in a welter of hard work and so did
the afternoon. Dr Thackery had visited the ward while
Clotilde was at lunch, too, which for some reason
annoyed her, although Sally had dealt quite competently
with his requirements and noted his instructions.
Getting the details from her staff nurse, she asked: 'Was
Dr Evans there too?'

Sally gave her a surprised look; she had been half
way through an intake and output chart and obviously
Sister Collins hadn't been listening. 'Yes, she was,
making sheep's eyes and calling him Sir with every
breath. She's had her hair permed, and I swear she's
wearing a padded bra. She needs it too!'

Just for a split second they weren't sister and staff

nurse, engrossed in medical matters, but young ladies with highly satisfactory curves of their own, exchanging satisfied glances, mingled with pity for Dr Evans who hadn't any curves to speak of.

They smiled, then Clotilde asked: 'About Mrs Gregson's false teeth—have they been found? She's very absentminded, you know, she leaves them all over the place. Get the nurses on another search, will you?'

Dr Evans came on to the ward just before tea time. 'Dr Thackery wants a blood sugar done on Mrs Dent,' she told Clotilde without bothering to say hullo. 'I suppose I'll have to cope on my own?'

'I'm afraid so.' Clotilde, mindful of her good intentions, made her voice friendly, at the same time looking at the hair; definitely permed and unless she was very mistaken, tinted. And Sally had been quite right about the bra.

Dr Evans turned away. 'Oh, I'll manage,' she said ungraciously, and then with a swift glance at Clotilde: 'I shall be seeing Dr Thackery this evening, anyway—for drinks.'

And blood samples? thought Clotilde naughtily, blood sugars in one hand and gin and tonic in the other? She watched the doctor walk down the ward and wondered what James could see in her. The thought nagged at her several times, but she had too much to do to give it any attention.

She went off duty at six o'clock an hour late, but since she didn't intend to do anything that evening, she didn't particularly mind. She would wash her hair and have a long, very hot bath, make tea and toast over in the Home, and go to bed with the day's newspapers. She was almost at the bottom of the staircase when she met Dr Thackery coming up, two at a time.

He stopped when he reached her and she perforce stopped too.

'You're late off duty. I phoned the Home and they said you were still on the ward. Anything urgent?'

She shook her head. 'No, just work. Mrs Dent's better ... Dr Evans has taken a blood sugar.' She watched his face; it was as calm as always, but of course he wasn't a man to show his feelings.

He said in an absentminded manner: 'Good, good. Could we have a meal together? To get this trip to Leyden sorted out. In an hour, or is that rushing you?'

'Not me, but won't it rush you? Dr Evans told me she was having drinks with you.'

His heavy lids open and she saw how very bright blue his eyes were.

'The devil—I'd forgotten! It's Jeff Saunders' birthday and he's asked most of the medical staff to have drinks with him in the common room. I don't need to stay for more than half an hour, though . . .' He looked at her in a puzzled way. 'Why on earth am I having drinks with Mary Evans? It's the last thing I want to do.'

'Is it?' asked Clotilde happily. 'Well, that's what she said, so naturally I thought . . .'

'If you thought that you're out of your mind, my girl. Now go and put on something pretty and we'll go to a pub.'

She assumed that James' idea of a pub might not be the same as Bruce's had been, so she played safe with a wool dress and the fur jacket her father had given her for the previous Christmas. And just as well, because he took her to Le Gavroche, which wasn't a pub at all, but a very upper-crust French restaurant.

He seemed in no hurry to discuss the trip to Leyden and she was content to enjoy the desultory talk, but over coffee he said: 'About Leyden, can you manage four days off?' He gave her the dates and she nodded.

'Yes, I think so—I'll take two week's days off together; it'll be a weekend, won't it? How do we go?'

'Drive down to Dover and cross to Calais.'

'Oh,' she visualised a map of France, 'really? Surely that's miles from Leyden? And do we go by train from there? Isn't it rather a long way?'

'We'll drive up,' he told her, and didn't offer any more information than that, leaving her speculating as to whether the Bentley went with them on the ferry—surely not? But of course cars went on the ferries and it would be far quicker. Having settled that point she ventured further.

'Do I stay with Katrina?' She asked.

'My grandparents live near Leyden—they'll be delighted to have you.' He added: 'Katrina spends a lot of time with them.'

'And you'll be with your friends?'

'The dreary old professors?' He laughed a little. 'We usually get together.'

'You're quite sure Katrina wants me to come? After all, we've only known each other a very short time.'

He smiled at her. 'Kitty phoned me this afternoon to remind me to see you about the trip and make sure that you were coming.'

'Oh, of course—how nice of her.' Colitilde smiled back and spoke lightly, wondering at the same time why the idea that he had asked her out in order to carry out Katrina's wishes and not for reasons of his own should depress her. She added in a voice of calm good sense: 'Is there anything else I should know about the journey? I have a passport—shall I want Dutch money?'

'Don't bother for those few days—if you want to buy

anything I'll let you have the gulden and you can pay me later.'

'You're very kind.' She hesitated and then voiced the question which had been at the back of her mind, nagging her. 'James, you're not asking me because—well, because you're sorry for me?' She had grown rather pink, but she gave him a straight look.

'No, that hadn't occurred to me.' He spoke calmly and she believed him.

'Oh, good—you don't mind me asking? I—I had to know . . .'

'I don't mind in the least. I should hope that by now we're able to be frank with each other. Do you skate, by the way? It might be cold enough in Holland.'

They talked trivialities after that until Clotilde said she would really have to get back to St Alma's. 'I'm on in the morning,' she reminded him, 'and it's your round, and you've no idea of the hustle and bustle that goes on until the moment you open the doors . . .'

'And you say "Good morning, sir" with a calm which I now know is grossly deceptive. Probably the last protesting patient has just been thrust willynilly back into bed.'

Clotilde giggled. 'As a matter of fact, it is rather like that—not always, but we have a lot of fraught moments.'

He drove her back presently and they bade each other a friendly goodnight at the hospital entrance. They would see each other on the ward in the morning, thought Clotilde, but that wasn't the same and he hadn't suggested meeting again. Probably she wouldn't see him to speak to as a friend before they went to Holland. Oh, well, she consoled herself as she made her way over to the home, that wasn't so far off.

She had a nasty feeling in her bones as she went on duty the next morning that the day wouldn't go well, and she was right. The junior night nurse had gone off sick during the night and there had not been anyone to replace her, so that the night staff nurse had left a good many of the humbler chores not done. Clotilde couldn't blame her; she had done the best she could, but there was a good deal of extra work to get through before the consultant's round, added to which two specimens which had been specially asked for had been thrown out by an over-enthusiastic junior nurse. Two of the more excitable ladies were then sick the moment they had clean sheets on their beds, and Mrs Gregson's teeth were missing yet again. Somehow they scrambled through the morning's work and Clotilde, outwardly serene but busy rehearsing a conciliatory speech about the specimens, whipped to the door just as Dr Thackery walked in.

He greeted her exactly as he always did, with polite impersonal friendliness, and she replied in the same manner before wishing the various members of his entourage a good morning. They all answered her except Dr Evans, who scowled and muttered, but since Dr Thackery was already advancing to his first patient he missed that and began at once to enquire of the lady in the bed how she was feeling.

They were more than halfway round and everything was going smoothly, and Clotilde relaxed. True, she and Dr Evans had had a couple of ladylike skirmishes over the diabetics' diets to which Dr Thackery had listened imperturbably, but things should now be plain sailing—there was the patient whose specimens had so unfortunately been disposed of, but since there had been no major snags so far, she had high hopes of glossing the business over. Hopes dashed, as she might have known, by Dr Evans, who having reminded Dr Thackery about them—quite unnecessarily—stood gloating as Clotilde explained briefly and with no excuses. 'Entirely my fault,' she observed calmly. 'I should have made sure that the nurses had known about them.'

'Inefficient,' muttered Dr Evans in a piercing whisper. 'Such a badly run ward—why, when I need a nurse to help me there's never one available . . .'

The doctor's long arm waved her to silence. 'You're short-staffed, Sister?' he wanted to know.

'A night nurse went off sick, sir, and there was no replacement. My nurses have done the very best they could.'

He nodded. 'I'm sure of that, Sister. Perhaps you'll see that the specimens are obtained as soon as possible? I don't think any blame can be attached to you or your nurses. The circumstances must have been trying.'

'Oh, they were,' agreed Clotilde. 'Round morning, you see.'

'Of course,' he smiled very faintly, his blue eyes twinkling. 'And now this next lady—Mrs Dawes—I haven't seen her yet, have I? If I might have her notes . . .'

The round finished and the whole party crowded into the office for coffee, while the more serious cases were discussed. The only one who took no part was Dr Evans, who sulked unless Dr Thackery addressed her directly, when she was instantly all smiles. It was really very unfortunate, thought Clotilde, that the woman disliked her so much. The nurses didn't like Dr Evans either– she bullied them when she thought no one was listening, and never a day passed without her seeking

Clotilde out so that she might grumble about something or the others. Her appointment was for six months and there were still four weeks to go, thought Clotilde gloomily.

The conference over and coffee drunk, everyone left, with Clotilde seeing them to the door as custom dictated, and this time Dr Thackery didn't come back. She watched his massive frame disappear into Men's Medical with a feeling of regret which she instantly squashed, since there was no reason for it, and she had a great deal on her mind anyway. She swept down the ward, taking Sally with her, so that they could go over the cases together and make sure they had all the instructions correct.

'And for heaven's sake, get those specimens and lock them up or something! He was very nice about it, but I wouldn't like to repeat a mistake like that.'

'He's always nice,' said Sally. 'What was Dr Evans on about? I couldn't quite hear.'

Clotilde told her. 'I can't think why she hates me so thoroughly.'

'Well, I can—just you stand beside her in front of a mirror! Besides, she's barmy about Dr Thackery.' Sally added delicately: 'Someone saw you coming in last night, Sister. It'll be all over the grapevine by this evening.'

Clotilde gave her staff nurse a limpid look. 'I spent the day with Dr Thackery's sister and he brought me back after dinner. We went shopping and she bought enough clothes to last the likes of us a lifetime. But she's a poppet, you can't help liking her.' She smiled suddenly. 'You can feed that into the grapevine if you get the chance!'

'Oh, I will.' Sally looked as though she was going to

say something else, but she didn't. I can hear the dinner trolleys, do you want me to start or will you come out, Sister?'

'I'll come; there are those low fat diets to sort out and if Mrs Gregson's teeth haven't been found, she'd better have the mince . . .'

Her mind was once more taken up with the ward and its occupants. James had become a vague friendly figure at the back of her busy mind.

The rest of the week went fast and beyond his ward visits she saw nothing of James. She worked all through the next week, saving her days off for the following weekend when they would be going to Holland. She was beginning to feel a little doubtful now, probably because he had made no more mention of it, and she wondered, not for the first time, if he was regretting his invitation. The second round of the week had come and gone without a word from him and in two days' time she was supposed to be going. She wondered wildly if she should phone him, but that would look pushing and she couldn't bring herself to do it. Perhaps she had made a mistake in the dates? Here she was, her passport ready, clothes suitable—she hoped—for the visit, cleaned and pressed and ready to pack. She even rang Rosie and asked if there had been any messages for her. There hadn't, of course; she listened to Rosie's cheerful voice speculating about the new owner of the house, giving her a résumé of Tinker's day, telling her about Bingo in the church hall, and then with the promise that she would be home again in ten days or so, Clotilde rang off. There was still the business of the furniture to settle and when she got back, she would have to decide once and for all what she was going to do.

She was filling in the diet sheet the next morning, one

ear tuned in to the familiar noises on the ward, when James walked in. He came silently so that she jumped a little with surprise.

'We don't seem to have seen much of each other,' he observed cheerfully. 'You're ready for Friday—tomorrow?'

She raised her lovely eyes to his placid face. 'Yes, but I thought you might have changed your mind . . .'

He sat on the edge of the desk, pushed her carefully piled charts carelessly on one side and said: 'Clotilde, I never change my mind. Now this is how we go—you're off duty tomorrow evening?'

'Yes.'

'Good. Can you be ready to leave around six o'clock—we can be on the other side by ten o'clock and drive straight to Leyden.'

'Yes, I'll be ready. I thought we weren't going until the next morning?'

He studied her for a minute under drooping lids. 'I don't want to waste a minute,' he told her.

He got up from the desk and all the charts slid on to the floor. He swept them into a heap and dumped them back again. He said: 'Katrina's very excited,' and when Clotilde looked up at him, bent and kissed her. He had gone as quickly and silently as he had come, leaving her to spend a frenzied half hour getting the charts in their proper order again.

CHAPTER SIX

THEY were well on the way to the ferry when Clotilde said carefully: 'There's quite a lot of gossip . . .'

'About us? Naturally there would be. You don't mind? It's silly enough to be ignored.'

She agreed quickly, a little put out at this matter-of-fact tone. 'Oh, of course, and it's only because it's—it's so soon after Bruce went away.'

'You still think of him, Clotilde?' The question was casual.

'Sometimes,' she admitted. 'But I try not to. That's all over and done with.' She wasn't going to say any more; there was nothing more tiresome than having to listen to someone else's troubles at the wrong time and in the wrong place, and at the moment it was definitely both. 'I expect Millie will miss you, and your other dog . . .'

'Both in the country with my parents,' he told her. 'George spends most of his time there, we go for long walks at the weekends.'

A tiny bit more about his private life, she tucked it away at the back of her mind and stored it with the other sparse titbits about him. She sat silent for a few minutes, trying to think of a leading question which would tell her a little more, but he began to talk about Holland and presently about France and Italy, both of which countries she had visited, the subject kept them pleasantly occupied until they reached Dover.

The crossing was uneventful, extremelyso for James, having provided her with a drink and made sure that she had something to read, went to sleep, which surprised her very much at first, but when she studied his face she could see how tired he was, with lines etched deeply on either side of his handsome nose. Undoubtedly he had had little sleep, and when he woke presently she taxed him with it.

'Were you up all night?' she wanted to know. 'Why didn't you put the trip off until tomorrow? You must be dog tired—I'm going to ask for some coffee for you.'

He sat up, his face magically its bland self once more. 'Now that's really kind of you, Clotilde. What a sensible young woman you are! You could be forgiven for flouncing off in a rage.'

She turned from ordering coffee. 'Why should I do that?' she asked. 'And were you up all night?'

'A good deal of it, yes. Don't worry—I'm quite able to drive.'

She eyed him calmly. 'I never supposed you weren't.' She smiled suddenly. 'I think you're able to do anything you want to do.'

He said gravely: 'A very encouraging remark, Clotilde—I must remember that.'

It was quite dark when they began their journey from Calais to Leyden. James had suggested that they didn't stop on the way. 'It's round about two hundred and fifty miles,' he explained, 'and a good road all the way, so we shall, with luck, be there by midnight.'

In actual fact it took less than that. The Bentley, given her head cut though distance like a knife through butter. For most of the way they travelled in a companionable silence, and once Clotilde dozed off and woke with a start to hear James chuckle. 'Not long now,' he told her. 'Those lights ahead are Leyden, Huis Asdaadt is a mile or so further on.'

'That's a strange name,' she commented.

'My mother's maiden name.'

'When you're here—in Holland, do you feel Dutch?'

'Oh, completely. But don't worry, we shall all speak English to you.'

He had slowed the car through the streets of Leyden and Clotilde did her best to see something of the small city, lights glimmering on water, steeple rooftops, narrow streets, lights from a few cafés still open and a handful of people on the streets. They were leaving the main roads now and the city behind them. 'We're going to the lakes to the north of Leyden,' said James, and she could hear the contentment in his voice. 'About two miles.'

Away from the town it was difficult to see anything. Now and again the car lights picked out a farmhouse or cottages, but no lights showed. When James turned the car between tall gateposts she was taken by surprise, and still more so when round a curve in the drive she saw the welcoming lights streaming from the dark mass of the house at its end.

There were shallow wide steps leading to the front door, which was opened as they reached it by a rotund little man with a fringe of white hair and a wide smile. He shook the doctor's hand and James said something to him which made him chuckle richly. 'This is Bas,' he told Clotilde. 'He's known me since I was a small boy, he keeps an eye on things here.'

Clotilde shook hands and murmured, and Bas said in rather strangely accented English: 'You are most welcome, miss,' and led the way across the hall, large and lofty with an oak staircase to one side of it. He opened double doors and ushered them into a room as lofty as the hall; a very splendid room, beautifully furnished. Clotilde had speculated idly about their destination, but she hadn't imagined anything quite as vast or magnificent, and she threw James a reproachful glance as they went in.

He ignored it, but she could see that he was amused and if they had been alone she might have had something to say about it, but they weren't—two chairs drawn up to the wood fire in the massive hearth were occupied. Their occupants got up as they crossed the room, a tall old man, stooping a little but still remarkably handsome and a small round lady with white hair dressed severely in an old-fashioned bun and wearing a pleated dress of some soft grey material which floated round her as she trotted to meet them.

The doctor bent to kiss her and then swung her up to kiss her again. Whatever he said made her chuckle delightedly before he put her gently on to her feet again. 'Oma, this is Clotilde.' He added with bland deliberation: 'Katrina's friend.' He smiled at Clotilde. 'My grandmother—her English is excellent.'

He left them together while he shook hands with the old man and then introduced him in turn. They stood talking for a few minutes before Mevrouw van Asdaadt urged them into the dining room, another vast room on the other side of the hall, where there was supper elegantly arranged on the oval table. Clotilde, who had thought that she was too sleepy to be hungry, found she was wrong. They sat, she and James, making a splendid meal of soup, light-as-air vol-au-vents, toasted sandwiches and creamy coffee, while the two elderlies sat, one at each side of them, plying them with more food and asking quesions about their journey and their plans.

'Well, I shall take Clotilde into Leyden tomorrow

morning, so she can meet Kitty—they'll want to look around then, I imagine, and that'll give me time to do some business for Mother. I'll bring them back for lunch if I may, and that will fit in very nicely with an afternoon appointment I have at the hospital.'

Clotilde, listening to this, felt vaguely put out—unjustifiably so, she had to admit. It was Katrina who had invited her to come, not James; he had merely given her a lift there and back, and she could hardly expect him to spend his days with her. She declared that his plans sounded delightful, and when Mevrouw van Adaasdt suggested that she might like to go to her bed, agreed willingly, wished them all goodnight and followed her hostess out of the room. The doctor, who had got up to open the door for them, kissed his grandmother as she passed him. 'As beautiful as ever,' he declared, and then kissed Clotilde too, but without comment.

'Such a dear boy,' said his grandmother, leading the way upstairs. 'I'm glad he has decided to marry at last.' She didn't give Clotilde time to comment upon this, which was just as well, because she was too surprised to say anything. 'You're in this room, my dear,' went on the old lady. 'If you want anything, there's a bell by the bed and someone will bring you tea in the morning.' She offered a cheek for Clotilde to kiss and smiled very sweetly at her. 'You're a very nice girl,' she observed in a satisfied voice and trotted out of the room, leaving Clotilde to inspect her surroundings.

Very luxurious they were too. A small brass bedstead with a canopy above it, a dressing table with a chintz petticoat, two small chairs upholstered in the same chintz, a vast wall cupboard to house a film star's wardrobe, and a pale carpet to sink her feet into. There was a bathroom too, pastel coloured to match the bedroom and lavishly fitted out with everything she might possibly need. Even her case had been unpacked and her nightie left ready on the bed. She had a hot bath and fell into bed. There was a pile of magazines and a book or two on the bedside table, but she was too tired to read. She lay in the dark, listening to the silence, and almost at once fell asleep.

James drove her into Leyden after breakfast the next morning, saw her into the delighted care of Katrina and drove off again.

'Always going somewhere,' grumbled Katrina. 'Come and see the rest of the flat. It's nice, isn't it? I live here during the term time, but I go to Grandmother's each weekend.'

It was a charming place—the top floor of a narrow house close to the University, with a large rather untidy living room, a small bedroom and a tiny bathroom and kitchen.

'Poky, isn't it?' said Katrina cheerfully. 'I couldn't bear to live in a small house, I'll have to marry someone with plenty of money ... wouldn't you rather live with plenty of space?'

Clotilde thought of her home, by no means as grand as Mevrouw van Asdaadt's but nonetheless comfortably spacious, and, regrettably, no longer hers to live in. And hard on the heels of her thought, she had a clear memory of James's house in London. Small it might be, but comparatively speaking, one could live in such a place without feeling in the least cramped. 'Your grandfather and grandmother have a lovely house,' she observed.

'Yes, it's pretty nice, isn't it? Father has a house too, you know—I suppose James will inherit it.'

She was busy making coffee in the kitchen, talking over her shoulder to Clotilde in the living room. Clotilde hoped she would say where the house was, but she didn't, and asking might sound nosey. They drank their coffee, and then got into their coats and went out into the wintry morning.

There was more than enough to see in Leyden. Indeed, after half an hour or so Clotilde came to the conclusion that even if she returned on the following day, she would have barely skimmed its historical buildings.

Katrina was a good companion and an excellent guide. They went first to the University and then the Lakenhal Museum, Pieterskerk, and lastly the Burcht, a mound of earth with a mediaeval fortification on its top. Katrina was a bit vague about its origin: 'But James will know—we'll ask him. What a pity there isn't more time. I promised I'd meet him outside the Medical School at half past twelve. He'll take us back to lunch. I'll have to come in tomorrow morning to pack some things—you'll come too, won't you? We might have time to see the shops.'

James was waiting for them. 'You must have a good influence on Kitty,' he observed. 'I usually wait for at least half an hour, and here you are barely five minutes late. Jump in the back, Kitty. Clotilde can sit beside me and tell me what she thinks of Leyden.'

'Wonderful, only I've had a kind of Reader's Digest of it; I could have spent hours just goggling at rooftops. Katrina's a marvellous guide, though, I think I've had a quick look at almost everything.'

He said at his most placid: 'You'll have to come again,' one of those annoying remarks which people make and don't mean, thought Clotilde, and went guiltily pink when he added: 'And that's no idle remark.'

Lunch was a cheerful meal and they were still sitting talking over their coffee when James declared that he would have to go. 'Back in time for drinks,' he told his grandmother as he left. 'Sorry about that, but it's a splendid opportunity to see one or two people . . .'

The afternoon passed remarkably quickly. Clotilde was taken on a tour of the house while her host and hostess took a nap. Katrina led her in and out of rooms and up and down passages, talking all the time. 'When we were little we always came here for school holidays—of course, James was already at medical school by the time I was old enough to come. He was my favourite—still is, although he's fourteen years older than I am. I see him much more often. Dilys is married, so is Peter, he's next after James—he lives in Scotland now, he's a doctor too, and Andrew is in Canada, he's a physicist. But we all meet for Christmas. Oma and Opa come to England and we have a house full—it's such fun! What will you do at Christmas, Clotilde?'

'I shall be on duty.' Clotilde spoke with a cheerfulness she didn't feel. 'We decorate the wards, you know, and the surgeons carve the turkey and we pay visits and the visitors have tea. Oh, and we sing carols on Christmas Eve.'

Katrina looked at her with something like horror. 'Don't you put on pretty clothes and go out—dancing and the theatre and dinner . . .?'

'Well, there's not much time for that,' said Clotilde almost apologetically. 'When we're off duty, we go out, of course.'

She remembered last Christmas. She and Bruce had gone out after she had gone off duty and had had a

meal in a funny little restaurant in Soho. She had been
very happy; she wondered briefly if she would ever be
happy like that again. Probably not, so she must be
thankful for what she had had. She said with genuine
cheerfulness this time: 'Tell me what you do. It must be
fun with a large family.'

'Oh, it is! Mother and Father . . .' Katrina stopped on
a quick breath. 'Oh, Tilly, I'm so sorry—I forgot, just
for a moment, you know. I don't suppose you want to
hear—I mean, it must hurt you . . .'

'But I'd like to hear, just the same,' prompted
Clotilde gently. 'Do you have any Dutch customs at
Christmas, or is it the same in both countries?'

They chatted idly as they went round the old house
and presently went down to tea, to sit talking to
Mevrouw van Asdaadt while her husband went away to
his study. He was writing a book, Clotilde was told. He
had been an eminent surgeon in his time and now, in
his early eighties, he was writing his reminiscences. 'So
many medical men in the family,' declared Mevrouw
van Asdaadt, 'for James's father is a physician, you
know, and so is Peter, I have gleaned enough
knowledge from them to set up a practice on my own
account!' She smiled widely. 'Though I do not look like
a doctor, I think.'

Katrina jumped up and gave her a hug. 'You look
like a super grandmother, Oma, and that's much nicer.'

It had been a lovely evening, Clotilde decided, lying
sleepily in her comfortable bed in the quiet house.
James had returned as they were sitting with their
drinks before dinner, and she had been glad she had
changed into a patterned silk jersey dress in soft browns
and coral, for he had looked at her with approval and
said in his placid way: 'That's nice—it suits you.'

Hardly an extravagant compliment, but for some reason she had been delighted with it. And dinner had been fun, with a lot of lighthearted talking into which she was skilfully drawn by him. She hadn't noticed that at the time, but now, with hindsight, she did. James was good at putting people at their ease. Her thoughts strayed away from the evening. His grandmother had said he was going to marry, and Clotilde wondered who the girl was and why there was no mention of her. Perhaps she lived in another part of the country or, more likely, near his parents' home. She would dearly like to know, but somehow she hesitated to ask James. He might snub her—very nicely, but snub her just the same. At least they were friends now and she hoped they would remain that way for a long time to come.

She thought drowsily that it would be nice to see him happily married. He would be a splendid husband, with the added bonus of good looks and enough money to make life very pleasant. He would be a super father too; but of course he would need a house outside London, large enough to accommodate his family but near enough for him to commute each day . . . She dozed off before deciding where that would be.

At breakfast James observed that he was entirely at their disposal all day.

'Oh good!' Katrina beamed at him over her coffee cup. 'Then you can drive us into Leyden and I'll finish my packing, then I can lock up the flat and come back here for the night, can't I, Oma?' She bit into a roll, then added: 'While I'm packing, James, you could take Tilly for a walk along Rapenburg and tell her about our famous siege.'

'Delighted,' murmured her brother, 'provided that it won't bore Clotilde.'

'Me, bored? Of course not, but perhaps there's something you want to do?'

He shook his head. 'Nothing—we might visit the Hortus Botanicus too. Very improving!' He twinkled nicely at her and she laughed.

'You're bent on improving my mind. I'd love to go.'

'And I hope you will all be my guests this evening. We shall have to leave tomorrow Grandmother, about two o'clock. You will be flying over for Christmas, of course? I'll meet your plane.'

Listening to these cheerful family arrangements, Clotilde felt a pang of regret; to be one of a large happy affectionate family seemed to her to be the epitome of happiness. She gave herself a mental shake; self-pity never did anyone any good, and she had a lot to be thankful for.

She caught James's eyes and smiled widely, anxious to let him see how much she was enjoying herself.

And as a matter of fact, as the day unfolded itself, she did enjoy herself very much. James deposited Katrina at her flat, arranged to meet her for coffee in the town in a couple of hours' time, parked the car and set off to show Clotilde the beauties of Rapenburg. And as they walked briskly beside its steely cold water, he told her about the siege in the sixteenth century and how ever since the lifting of that seige had been marked by the eating of fish and loaves of white bread, and it was because of that siege that the city had been granted a university by William the Silent.

Clotilde looked at the building, ringed around the quad with lecture halls, library and the famous garden, and wanted to know if James had studied there.

'Yes, I took my degree here and then went to Cambridge—that pleased both sides of the family.'

'But you like living in England?' She asked a little anxiously.

'Of course. I was educated there, and although I come to Holland frequently I'm Dorset born and bred.'

She just stopped herself in time from asking whereabouts in Dorset. 'The best of both worlds,' she observed brightly.

It was a cold raw morning, but she didn't notice that. They explored the Hortus Botanicus and she was quite astonished when James reminded her that they were to meet Katrina. And over coffee, Katrina declared that she surely had to have a new pair of boots and Clotilde must go with her to buy them. 'We'll be half an hour,' she told James, 'so go and talk to one of your professors . . .' She broke off as a pretty young woman with gleaming golden hair under a little fur hat came across the cafe to their table. 'Better still,' said Katrina softly, 'here's Hortense. Chat her up, James—you've been neglecting her shamefully.'

'Such a good idea'. He showed no sign of discomfiture and his voice was as placid as ever. He got to his feet. 'You two run off, then—I'll be in the University car park in an hour's time.' He turned a smiling face to the girl. 'Hortense, how delightful! Sit down and have coffee and I'll have another cup to keep you company . . .'

'An old girl-friend,' said Katrina as she and Clotilde reached the pavement. 'And she's never given up hope—she hasn't got a chance, though. James has fallen hook, line and sinker for someone at St Alma's.' She spoke in a guileless voice and glanced at Clotilde. 'Did you know that?'

'Well, no, but I don't see much of James at St

Alma's—I mean, he's a consultant—he does his rounds on the ward and tells me what he wants done . . .'

'But he doesn't discuss his love life with you?'

Clotilde said in a shocked voice: 'Good gracious, I should think not!' and then: 'Though I'm sure he has one.'

'Oh, he's always had girl-friends, but he's never wanted to get married until now—it's all very—how do you say it? Hush-hush. He's very good at keeping it dark, and then suddenly you'll all be surprised . . .'

It must be Mary Evans, thought Clotilde, for the entire hospital would fall over backwards with astonishment. Perhaps the girl had a hidden something no one else had noticed. Certainly it must be something with more appeal than a padded bra. 'What a tearing shame,' said Clotilde forcefully, and realised with horror that she had spoken out loud. 'That none of us are able to guess,' she finished hastily.

'Oh well,' observed Katrina cheerfully, 'he'll tell you in his own time. He never was one to show his feelings.'

With which remark, upon reflection, Clotilde was bound to agree.

The three of them drove to Katwijk-aan-zee after lunch and walked along the wide stretch of sand in the teeth of a bitter wind, with grey clouds scudding low above their heads, before having tea at one of the hotels, now almost empty, on the boulevard, and in the evening they all went into Leyden and had dinner at the Rotisserie Oudt Leyden; smoked eel for starters, roast pheasant with an array of vegetables, and gigantic and very ornate icecreams for dessert. And since it was something of an occasion, they drank champagne, then sat around drinking coffee until late in the evening. A lovely dinner, mused Clotilde, getting ready for bed, sad at the thought that it was the last evening there. She was happy in the charming old house and she liked James's grandparents; not for one moment had she ever felt a stranger there, she had been accepted and absorbed into the family circle quite effortlessly. Despite the grandeur of their surroundings, the old people lived a simple, placid, contented life. True, they had all that they could possibly wish for, but since, presumably, they had had that all their lives, they merely accepted it in a matter-of-fact manner. In two days' time she would be back at St Alma's, drinking strong tea with her friends and gossiping over the days' work. And when she got back, she reflected, she would have to go home, choose the furniture she needed, and go over the list of things to be sold which doubtless Mr Trent would have ready by now. Something she dreaded but which had to be done.

They did nothing much the next day. James had to go into town once again, but this time he didn't offer to take them with him. They passed the morning happily enough and by the time they had lingered over lunch, it was time to leave. The journey back wasn't all that like the one coming. Katrina, sitting in front with her brother, talked for most of the time. She was a delightful companion, and Clotilde was surprised to find they were back in Calais. The crossing was a different matter; the sea was uncommonly rough and Katrina retired to a cabin for the whole of the short crossing, leaving Clotilde to keep James company, which meant that they sat comfortably reading, barely exchanging a word, perfectly at ease with each other.

Once on dry land Katrina regained her vivacity, talking nineteen to the dozen, planning what she would do when she got home, wanting to know what Clotilde was going to do.

'Go to bed,' said Clotilde with her usual good sense. 'I'm on duty in the morning.'

'Oh, my poor Tilly, while I am home you must come and see me. James can drive you down when he comes. For Christmas, perhaps?'

'That's sweet of you,' said Clotilde quickly before James felt that he must add his voice to the invitation, 'but I'm on duty over Christmas—we always are, you know.'

'Then before Christmas,' persisted Katrina.

'I really can't,' declared Clotilde, knowing that if James had added his voice to his sister's she would have found a way. But he didn't, so she added: 'I have to go home and decide what furniture I'm to keep and see about Rosie—that's the housekeeper. I shall need all my free days to get everything settled.' She changed the conversation quickly, anxious to get away from her own affairs, suddenly terrified that James would offer to help in some way, not because he really wanted to but because he felt that he should. 'How long are you staying in England? I expect you go to a lot of parties while you're here.'

Katrina was easily diverted. She enlarged at some length on the pleasures in store and was earnestly discussing the merits of a ballerina-length dress as opposed to a slim sheath her mother thought was too old for her, when James swept into St Alma's forecourt and stopped.

It took Katrina all of five minutes to say goodbye while James sat patiently, but finally he got out, opened the door for Clotilde and reached for her case. It was only a stone's throw to the door. She began on her little speech of thanks before they reached it, gabbling rather because she had the nasty feeling that he was anxious to be gone. He had probably been bored stiff for the whole journey, because he had hardly spoken, and the quicker she said goodbye the better. She held out a hand and thanked him again in a hurried voice not at all like her usual quiet calm one. His own quiet goodbye echoed in her ears as she went through the doors, picked up her case and hurried across the entrance hall without a backward glance.

A delightful episode, she told herself soberly as she got ready for bed, but only an episode. She would take care to avoid James as much as possible from now on, and that shouldn't be too difficult. On the ward he wasn't James at all, but Dr Thackery, and the hospital was large enough for her to nip out of sight if a chance encounter was likely. She turned her thoughts resolutely to her own problems, now imminent; she wouldn't have any days off for a week at least, and before then she must find time to go and see Mr Trent to make sure that everything was going ahead as he had hoped. She concentrated hard on a variety of knotty problems, but somehow her thoughts drifted back to James which was surprising, because after all he had nothing to do with her future.

Pushing open the door of the ward in the morning, she felt as though she had been away for weeks instead of a mere four days. She wished the patients a general good morning and went into her office, to be considerably cheered by the relieved faces of the night nurses and Sally. Their pleasure at seeing her back was comforting and she listened with an attentive ear to the report, asked a few sapient questions, sent the night nurses off duty, went briskly to make sure that the student nurses were dealing properly with breakfasts, then went back to her desk. Sally joined her almost at once with two cups of tea and a handful of notes.

'Odds and ends I thought you'd want to know about,' she explained, 'mostly requests for off duty, but there are one or two queries from relations and the dispensary want to see you about a prescription they can't account for, and the laundry . . .'

Clotilde made a face and Sally laughed. 'It's sheets this time—they say we've ordered too many during the last month and they'll have to cut down.'

Clotilde took a gulp of tea. 'We'll see about that. You've managed very well, Sally. You've got days off tomorrow, haven't you?'

The morning round took a long time. There were a handful of new patients and those she already knew kept her talking. She went down the ward back to her desk thinking that it didn't take long to slip back into harness again, and perhaps that was a good thing. The morning went in a flash and in the afternoon Dr Evans did a protracted round. She answered Clotilde's polite greeting sulkily and stared at her darkly. She must have known about Clotilde's trip to Holland, but she said nothing, only as she was on the point of going she remarked: 'I heard that you're thinking of leaving, Sister Collins. A change might be a good idea, don't you agree?'

'Perhaps,' agreed Clotilde serenely, 'but I haven't any definite plans yet.'

'There are some splendid jobs abroad for young women like you,' said Dr Evans. She made it sound like a threat. 'Dr Thackery was only saying last week that it would be best for you to start a new life somewhere else; I said I'd suggest it to you when I had a chance.'

Clotilde looked down at the other girl, taking comfort from the fact that she was several inches taller. She had no intention of losing her temper. Whether James had said that or no was something to be guessed at, but of one thing she was sure—he must be on very intimate terms with Mary Evans if he discussed the nursing staff with her. She knew he wasn't that kind of man, he wouldn't gossip around. She said sweetly: 'Why, thank you, Dr Evans for wanting to help me, I really must do some serious thinking. It's a pity Christmas is so close; that's such a busy time, but once it's over...' She left her sentence in mid-air for her companion to make what she liked of it.

She dismissed the distasteful conversation from her mind very firmly. If she thought about it for too long she would get angry, not only that, she would begin to wonder if James had really discussed her behind her back.

There was more than enough to keep her busy for the rest of the day, and by evening she was tired enough to go to bed after supper. Not that she went to sleep; a steady stream of friends popped in at intervals wanting to know what she had thought of Holland and what she had done while she was there. 'Did you see much of Dr Thackery?' they all asked inevitably.

And she answered with a fair amount of truth. 'He was away for most of the time, seeing people at the University, but his sister and I had a lovely time.' She recounted the more interesting aspects of Leyden to each enquirer in turn, and made a point of telling Fiona, who was, after all, one of her closest friends, that Dr Thackery had been kindness itself and that he would have done the same for anyone. 'He's helped me over such a bad patch,' she pointed out, 'and I shall always be so grateful to him.'

Fiona, eating the last of the biscuits in Clotilde's tin, said, 'Um,' rather indistinctly, and then: 'Have you decided to leave? Dr Evans told me this evening that it would be the best thing that you could do.' She glanced at Clotilde. 'She's a bitch,' she observed inelegantly. 'I think she hates us all.'

'And me in particular. I can't think why.'

Fiona looked as though she was going to say something, but she swallowed the last of the biscuit instead. 'Well, Tilly, I'm off to bed. See you in the morning. You do know that there's no consultant's round in the morning, don't you? Dr Evans told me.'

'I didn't know—I daresay she forgot. Jeff Saunders will be doing it instead?'

'Yes. Are you off in the evening? Let's go out to eat—most of us are off duty, we'll make up a party.'

'That's be fun. It will give us a chance to get together over Christmas.'

The days slid by, by the end of the week Clotilde felt as though she had never been away. Leyden was a dream which she had precious little time to remember and James had disappeared into thin air. She plunged into preparations for Christmas—ward decorations, extra food for the patients, off duty for the nurses, and on her first free morning, she went to see Mr Trent again.

He received her kindly, as he always did, assured her that everything was going exactly as it should and presented her with a list of the furniture which had been valued. The total surprised her, she had no idea that it would be so much; when she phoned Rosie, she had been told that two gentlemen had been and spent hours poking around the house, saying almost nothing, and Clotilde had gained the impression that they hadn't thought much of anything. She looked up at Mr Trent and asked: 'Isn't this an awful lot of money?'

'The value of the furniture, my dear—no more, no less. Your parents had some nice pieces. Remember that you still have to choose anything you wish to keep for yourself.'

She nodded. 'And Rosie? Has anything been said about her staying on?'

'I'm glad to say that the new owner wishes her to remain. I thought it best if you were to tell her when you see her.'

He shuffled some papers before him. 'I'm told that the new owner will not be taking up residence just yet, and he has instructed his solicitor to inform me that you are at liberty to visit Miss Hicks if you should wish to do so, and that the furniture you may choose to take may remain in the house until such time as you have found suitable accommodation for yourself.'

Clotilde looked at him doubtfully. 'I don't know what to do,' she confessed. 'I know I should have made up my mind by now and people keep telling me it would be best for me if I left St Alma's and started somewhere else miles away. What do you advise, Mr Trent?'

He took so long to reply that she thought perhaps he hadn't heard her. 'Give the matter a little more thought,' he said at length. 'Perhaps after Christmas? Meanwhile go ahead and choose the pieces you wish to keep, enquire about a new post if you wish to do so, but make no final decision. That is my advice, Clotilde, if you care to take it.'

'Oh, I will, Mr Trent and thank you.' She got up to

go. 'I'll come and see you again, shall I? when I've decided.'

James had missed two rounds by now and she hadn't been able to pluck up the courage to ask Jeff where he was. She hoped that the hospital had understood that his friendliness towards her had been because she had needed help rather badly, but now she was able to cope once more, and any interest she might show in him might start rumours; she didn't think they would be unkind, because as far as she knew she hadn't any enemies at St Alma's, but once the grapevine got going, however silly the tale, it was hard to squash.

She conducted the round with Jeff in exactly the same manner as if it were Dr Thackery, taking care to be ready for him, escorting him to the door, making sure that everything went without a hitch. Round day came again once more and she spent the first hour or so after breakfast preparing for it. Everything was in readiness and she went to her office. There were ten minutes or so left; she could start some paperwork. Only she didn't. She sat at her desk, staring out of the window at the grey morning, feeling empty of all feeling. She frowned; she must snap out of it. Still frowning, she looked over her shoulder as the door opened and James Thackery walked in.

CHAPTER SEVEN

CLOTILDE didn't feel empty any more; the world was suddenly a magic place, the morning was no longer grey. Only by the strongest effort of will did she stop herself from hurling herself at James, something which took so much of her powers that she had nothing to say at all.

'You look cross,' observed James, shutting the door behind him and leaning against it.

Clotilde took a grip on herself. 'No, oh no—just surprised.' It vexed her that her voice came out in a shaky squeak. She drew a deep breath and tried again with more success. 'You'll be doing the round, sir?'

'Correct, Sister Collins.' He leaned forward and kissed her lightly. 'Pleased to see me?' he wanted to know. 'And missed me?'

She had no intention of allowing her feelings to show. 'We are always glad to see you, sir,' she said sedately, 'and naturally you've been missed.'

She felt her cheeks grow warm under his amused look and wished him, without meaning it in the least, at the other side of the world—or at least far enough away for her to pull herself together. That wish at least was more or less granted.

'I'm going to Men's Medical first this morning,' he told her. 'I'll see you later.'

He had gone, closing the door silently behind him, and Clotilde sat staring at it, waiting for her heart to stop pounding and her thoughts to become coherent once more. A fine kettle of fish, she muttered savagely. What had happened to the cool, friendly relationship she had enjoyed with the doctor? Gone—and in no way could she see it returning. Falling in love with him had been the last thing she had expected to do—indeed, she had never entertained the idea, and here she was now, head over heels and in a fair way to making a fool of herself. But at least it would settle one question for her; to leave St Alma's as soon as she decently could. She sat back in her chair for a moment, allowing herself the luxury of thinking about James, pretending, for a few crazy seconds, that he had fallen in love with her too. And that's nonsense, she reminded herself, he's already in love with this mysterious girl, and could she be Mary Evans? Well, she would perhaps get a clue or two on the round.

She got up and went to inspect her face in the small mirror on the wall. She looked exactly the same as usual, which surprised her, although it was a relief too. With a great effort she put the last astonishing few minutes out of her head, and went into the ward.

It would be the best part of an hour before Dr Thackery would arrive. She sent two nurses to their coffee, told the other two to go when the other pair returned, and swept Sally back into the office.

'Let's have a quick cup before they get here,' she suggested. 'It's going to make dinners awfully late. Still, we're all on, aren't we? Two can tidy up and four of us can get the dinners served. Someone's off for a half day . . . You'd better all go to second dinner and I'll have something here.'

'Yes, Sister.' Sally poured the coffee and said hesitantly: 'You're feeling all right, Sister? You look flushed . . . are you starting a cold?'

'I feel fine, thanks.'

'Was Dr Thackery in a good mood? It's not like him to come here second. Did he say why?'

'No, I didn't ask him.' She had been dumb, swept away on a tide of suddenly discovered love. 'When do you want your days off next week? I don't mind in the least when I have mine—I shall be going home.' She told Sally about Rosie staying on as housekeeper. 'And you've no idea what a relief that is. How about applying for this job when I go, Sally?'

'You're not going—Sister, why? Must you? I mean, you've got lots of friends here and the patients dote on you, and Dr Thackery and you get on so well together.'

Clotilde let that pass. 'I must make a change, Sally— start again somewhere. The last month or so hasn't been too easy.' She smiled at Sally. 'But don't tell anyone yet, will you? You know what the grapevine's like.' She looked at her watch and jumped to her feet. 'We'd better get moving. Tell two of the nurses to keep close behind us as we go round and straighten the beds and so on. See that they understand that they must go about it stealthily. It'll save time once the round's over. They'll have had coffee over on the other side, though I suppose I'll have to offer it.'

The patients were restless. Round days were the bright spots in their week and they were being deprived of their small excitements. Clotilde went from one bed to the other, assuring the occupants that any minute now it would start, and to add weight to her words, went down the ward looking as cool and contained as she always did. She managed to stay that way, too, as the doors opened and Dr Thackery walked in. He wished her a grave good morning, just as though he hadn't already seen her not two hours since, hoped she

would forgive him for being so late, and started his
round, so exactly as he always was that she found
herself behaving in her usual calm way, answering his
questions readily, passing various forms when he asked
for them, listening carefully to his instructions. She felt
as though she were acting a part, while at the same time
she was outside herself, watching herself perform. And
over and above that she watched Mary Evans, sporting
a new hairstyle today and her white coat open over a
too tight sweater which did nothing to camouflage the
padded bra. She looked happy and excited, only taking
her eyes off James's face when she had to. And when
Clotilde offered coffee at the end of the round and the
doctor refused, she gave Clotilde a triumphant look as
they started off down the ward again, asking him
questions about the patients which he courteously
answered, pausing only long enough to bid Clotilde a
mild, 'Good morning, Sister.'

Clotilde stood at the door as she always did. She
looked capable and assured and serene, although the
serenity went abruptly enough when she glanced out of
the window a few minutes later and saw James and
Mary Evans sauntering along together deep in
conversation. Of course they might have been discussing
a patient . . . She turned her back and went into the
ward to serve the puddings.

Perhaps it was a good thing, she decided later, that
she had so much to do that there was precious little
time to think about anything else but her work. There
were quite a few ill women on the ward who needed
careful watching and two diabetics who weren't
stabilised yet. Clotilde gobbled a sandwich and drained
a pot of tea at her desk, then went back on to the ward.
Mrs Jeeves, who had been admitted with chest pains the

day before, was looking poorly; she had been meticulously examined that morning and James had changed the treatment Dr Evans had ordered on the previous evening; he had put her on half-hourly observations too and had given his opinion that the lady was cooking up something and that he was to be warned of any change.

Clotilde, coming away from the bed, met Sally, back from her dinner.

'Come into the office,' she suggested. 'We'll go over Dr Thackery's instructions about Mrs Jeeves. I'm not too happy about her—get someone right away if you're worried.'

She went off duty presently. She almost never took an afternoon off, but she wanted to get something for Rosie and there wouldn't be a chance to shop before she went home during the following week. Rosie needed a new, warm dressing gown, her old one was thin and shabby and a dreary grey, and Christmas was near enough for Clotilde to give it to her on her next visit. She took a slow-moving bus up Oxford Street and found what she wanted in Marks and Spencer's—bright red, cosily soft and thick. She bought red slippers to match too, and well satisfied with her purchases, made the tiresome journey back to St Alma's. There was just time for tea before she went back on duty.

Everyone was all right, Sally reported. The ill patients had had their various treatments and their conditions were unchanged and the diabetics, for a wonder, weren't loaded with sugar. 'I did a test half an hour ago and they were okay Mrs Jeeves is about the same . . .' She sounded doubtful and Clotilde said understandingly:

'I know—you can't put your finger on it, can you?

Something's not right.' She looked at the duty list. 'Who've I got on? Roberts and Symes . . . Night Staff Nurse has nights off, hasn't she? I wonder who's relieving her?'

Sally said cautiously: 'Well, Dawes is doing relief,' and grinned sympathetically. Staff Nurse Dawes was as pretty as a picture, with baby blue eyes and a cultivated lisp. She was sweet to her patients but was quite incapable of coping with any crisis which might arise. The junior housemen and the students adored her and the Ward Sisters tried every trick under the sun to avoid having her on their particular ward.

Clotilde sighed. 'Oh well,' she observed philosophically, 'we haven't had her for weeks, I suppose we mustn't grumble. Only I wish Mrs Jeeves wasn't such an unknown quantity.'

The evening's work went forward at a brisk pace. Clotilde went to her supper, came back and sent the nurses to theirs and took her report to finish by Mrs Jeeves's bed. She was sleeping lightly, but she was restless and her pulse was rising slowly. Clotilde finished the report and made up her mind to stay for a while after she had given the report; it would give the night nurses time to settle the patients down and when the ward was quiet, one of them could sit near Mrs Jeeves.

Staff Nurse Dawes appeared to be listening carefully to everything Clotilde read out to her. They did a round together, checking the ill patients and going last of all to Mrs Jeeves. As they went down the ward Clotilde said: 'I've the off-duty to make out, Staff. I'll sit by Mrs Jeeves while you and Nurse get the ward tucked up for the night.'

Mrs Jeeves was awake when she returned to the bed.

She looked anxious, and when Clotilde took her hand it was coldly clammy; she took a brief look at the cyanosed face on the pillow, smiled reassuringly, twitched the curtain behind her to give partial concealment and turned on the oxygen. 'You'll feel better when you've had some more air,' she said quietly. 'Try not to worry.' She called softly over her shoulder: 'Staff Nurse, will you come here?'

Staff Nurse Dawes's charming face appeared round the edge of the curtain; she gazed at Clotilde and then at Mrs Jeeves. She looked like a scared child. 'Draw the curtains,' said Clotilde briskly, 'then ring the Registrar and see if you can get him. Dr Evans will do if you can't get him, and please be quick about it.'

Staff Nurse Dawes hesitated maddeningly: 'Suppose they're not there? What shall I do? Shall I get Night Sister?' Her eyes slid to Mrs Jeeves, lying so still, struggling to breathe. 'Shall I send Nurse here, Sister?'

'Get me a doctor, Staff, and fast!'

Staff Nurse Dawes gulped and then gave a scared squeal as she was put on one side and James took her place. His eyes flickered over Clotilde before he bent over his patient. 'How long?' he asked.

'About three minutes ago; sudden onset with breathlessness and sweating. Mrs Jeeves has been sleeping on and off all the evening but restless at times. Her pulse has been going up very slightly.'

'Let's get the blood gases. Nurse has gone to phone, presumably. New, is she?'

'No, relief staff nurse.' Clotilde was checking her patient's pulse.

'On night duty, are you?'

'No, I stayed because I wasn't too happy.'

'Good girl.' He bent his long back and said in a kind

voice: 'You're going to feel better very soon, Mrs Jeeves. I'm going to give you an injection and we shall stay with you until it works.' He straightened up and said softly: 'Where the hell's that nurse? I'm going to give streptokinase. Have you any on the ward?'

'Yes, but only five hundred thousand units—you'll need more . . .'

'Get someone to go to the dispensary. Where's Night Sister?'

'On her first round—Children's Medical about now.' Clotilde broke off as Staff Nurse Dawes's face peered cautiously round the doctor's vast form.

'Dr Evans is coming, Sister.'

Clotilde nodded. 'Good. Staff, stay here with Dr Thackery while I get something from the D.D.A. cupboard. Can I have the keys?' She waited until Staff Nurse Dawes had taken her place. 'I'll get Night Sister at the same time.' She heard the hurrying feet and added: 'Here's Dr Evans.'

'What's all this?' demanded Dr Evans. 'I've been here twice this evening, can't you . . .? She came round the curtains and saw Dr Thackery. Clotilde would dearly have loved to to have waited to see what would happen next, but she slid away. She phoned Night Sister first, fetched the drug and everything necessary for its giving and went silently back to take over from Staff Nurse Dawes. The anticoagulant needed to be given over a half hour of time, a long time for someone fighting for their breath as Mrs Jeeves was going to fight for hers. Clotilde prayed that she would hold out so that the massive pulmonary embolism might dissolve, if not pulmonary embolectomy might be undertaken as a last hope.

Dr Evans was taking blood to estimate the gases, for once subdued in her manner. Clotilde heard a faint

rustle and an even fainter footfall and heard with relief
Night Sister's whisper behind her. They were good
friends, she and Jo Wills, and Jo wasn't a girl who
needed all the I's dotted and T's crossed.

'We'll need the Path Lab opened up—can you get
whoever's on call? And enough streptokinase to take us
round to the morning.'

She heard Jo's barely audible, 'okay,' and then: 'I'll
be back in five minutes, love.'

Which she was with an almost imperceptible nod to
Clotilde, she then took Staff Nurse Dawes's place by Dr
Evans. And all this while James had been giving the
anticoagulant, timed it exactly, sitting on the edge of
Mrs Jeeves' bed, totally relaxed, giving instructions
from time to time in his placid voice. It seemed a very
long time before he said quietly: 'I think we're winning,'
and indeed Mrs Jeeves was no worse; not much better
either but holding her own; if she could hang on until
the anticoagulant had a chance to do its work . . .

He spoke to Mary Evans, 'Get that blood down to
the Path Lab, they should be there by now, then I
suggest that you do your late round; we can manage
here for the moment,' and when she had gone,
reluctantly: 'Tilly and I can cope between us, Jo, but
will you come if we bleep? And is that blue-eyed girl,
capable of looking after this ward without yelping for
help?'

Clotilde and Jo exchanged speaking looks. It was, to
say the least of it, unusual for Dr Thackery to lose his
calm, and so often Staff Nurse Dawes had got away
with it; lisping prettily for help, fluttering her eyelashes
while she wriggled out of some tricky job.

'I'll see that she does,' said Jo, and winked at
Clotilde.

James hadn't taken his eyes off his patient. 'Just keep her out of my way,' he begged.

It was well after midnight when he said: 'Let's have the oxygen flow down and see how she is. If all's well, we'll get her over to Intensive Care. Please warn Night Sister, will you?'

It was an hour later before Clotilde crawled into bed. Mrs Jeeves safely bedded down in the Intensive Care unit. She had drunk a cup of tea in James's company, sitting in Jo's office, mumbled her good-nights, only too well aware that she was tired and cold and that reaction was making her pettish. James had thanked her gravely and told her, quite un-necessarily, to go to bed.

She was her contained, serene self the next morning. She ate her breakfast, laughed and chatted with her friends and went on duty to sit patiently while Staff Nurse Dawes gave her report, interlarded with asides about the awful night it had been.

'Well, we must expect these things to happen,' Clotilde pointed out. 'This is, after all, a hospital.'

'Yeth, Sister,' agreed her companion infuriatingly, and added: 'Dr Thackery was quite nasty; after all, I had the ward to look after.'

'At such times a doctor thinks only of his patient,' observed Clotilde. 'Are you on duty here this evening?'

'Yeth, Sithter. Mrs Jeeves won't be back? I'd need extra help . . .'

'No, I doubt if she'll return for a day or two.' Clotilde nodded dismissal, and watched the girl go down the ward on her way to breakfast and bed. She should have been a model or worked in a boutique. Clotilde wondered, not for the first time, how she had ever got into the nursing profession. Probably she would like to marry a doctor ... Which reminded her forcibly that that was exactly what she wanted to do herself.

She spent the next half hour with Sally, arranging the day's work, telling her about Mrs Jeeves, listening to Sally's mild grumbles about Staff Nurse Dawes's ideas about leaving a tidy ward. 'And she forgot to test the diabetics' specimens; I've held back their breakfasts.' She looked at Clotilde's face. 'You have had a rotten time—I'll get you a cup of tea. There's nothing to worry about at the moment.'

And at Clotilde's demur: 'That Dawes girl forgot to chart the temps.' She put the pile in front of Clotilde. 'If you must work, Sister, they'll keep you busy for ten minutes or so.'

Clotilde laughed, then picked up her pen and drew the first chart towards her, and at the same time the door was pushed wide and James came in.

The unexpectedness of it sent the colour flying into her cheeks, but her voice was nice and steady. He looked tired, as well he might be, but as immaculate as always. His good morning was cheerful: 'And I passed your staff nurse on her way to the kitchen. She's bringing me a cup too, I hope you don't mind?'

Clotilde pushed the charts aside. 'Of course not. Do you want anything to eat?' And when he shook his head: 'How's Mrs Jeeves?'

'Holding her own. Gave us a nasty turn, didn't it? What a good thing it was that you'd decided to stay on duty—that pretty blue-eyed charmer wasn't much good, was she?'

'Well, I daresay she hadn't seen a pulmonary embolism before—they're a bit scarey.'

Sally came in with the tea and he got up from the corner of the desk and took the cups from her with a smile. 'Happy to be back at work?' he asked.

Clotilde took a sip of tea. She said with false heartiness: 'Oh, yes—there are some interesting patients on the ward ...' She stopped before she said anything even more inane.

'No plans yet?' he asked. He picked up the off duty book and began to look through it.

'No—at least, not—not quite decided. I thought I'd get Christmas over first.'

'Very wise. When are you going home again?'

She had written up off duty for next week; he couldn't have seen it. She said lightly: 'I don't know. Rosie's very well, I phoned her.'

He got up from the desk, towering over her. 'I'm glad to hear that. Thanks for the tea.' He glanced at his watch. 'I've a date with Mary in five minutes, I'll be off.' At the door he looked back at her. 'Thanks for last night—Mrs Jeeves could have died so easily.'

Of one thing Clotilde was certain, she wasn't going to be able to stand seeing him much more; these casual friendly meetings were playing havoc with her feelings. She glanced out of the window, down below to the inner yard of the hospital, and there he was, walking across it with Mary Evans beside him. They could be going to see a patient, of course, but they went in the Surgical Wing door. She turned her back on them and buried her pretty nose in the charts.

She didn't see him for two days, and when he did come, it was for his round, hedged about by the group of people who always accompanied him. Clotilde led him from bed to bed, made concise reports about their occupants, made a careful note of his instructions, entertained him and his companions to coffee and at last saw them off the ward. She was surprised at herself, behaving just as she always did when all she really wanted to do was to throw herself into his arms. A good thing that she had days off and would be driving herself home that evening.

There was an icy rain falling as she left the hospital later. The dark afternoon had lapsed earlier than usual into a dark evening and the journey home would be a dreary one, but it was grand to be away from London, even for such a short time; she would spend her two days doing nothing much. Walking Tinker, choosing furniture, and making final plans for Christmas—the last not as difficult as it might sound, for she had spent several Christmases on Women's Medical and knew the routine by heart. Besides, while she did it she would be sitting cosily by the fire writing her neat lists.

Rosie was waiting for her with a hot supper and a warm welcome. Clotilde flung her outdoor things down in the hall, while Tinker almost knocked her off her feet with delight, then she sat down at the kitchen table. It was lovely to talk to Rosie; a far happier Rosie, she noted with relief, now that her future was safe. She had finished her soup and begun to eat the omelette before Rosie asked: 'What's the matter, Miss Tilly? I know you've had a good time seeing your friend in Holland, but things aren't right, are they?'

Clotilde looked down at her plate. 'Perhaps not quite, Rosie, but they'll work out. They always do. We've been busy and I expect I'm tired. I'll be fine after a good night's sleep. Tomorrow I'll go round picking out the bits and pieces I want to keep . . .'

'Yes, love, but where will you put them? Are you going to find somewhere to live away from that hospital? Perhaps whoever is coming here will let you store them—you know there's the attic and that big bedroom at the back that's never used.'

'He might want to use it,' observed Clotilde reasonably. 'Besides, he might not like me turning up after he's settled in and wanting to move my things out. I think I'd better get them stored—I'm not even sure what I want yet.' She poured tea for both of them. 'Enough to furnish a bedsitter, I suppose.'

She spilt the tea when Rosie asked suddenly: 'Do you see that nice Dr Thackery very often? Such a dear kind man, and his family sound nice too.'

'I see him when he does the ward round. He's—he's getting married soon, his sister told me. I have an awful feeling it's to his house doctor—a Welsh girl who has been angling for him for weeks. None of us like her, which is horrid of us, I suppose . . .' She launched into a light hearted description of Mary Evans to make Rosie laugh, and presently they cleared away their supper and went to bed. Clotilde lay awake for a long while, wondering what James was doing. Entertaining Mary to dinner in his charming house, no doubt, perhaps deciding on the date of the wedding.

The rain had ceased by the time she got up the next morning. She took Tinker for a run and then came back into the house, to go through it room by room trying to decide what she needed. Of course, it would be sensible to select useful furniture; small stuff that would fit into a flat or bedsitter. She had no idea if she would ever have either; she found it impossible to envisage anything but a vague, misty future in which a job and a home of her own seemed hopelessly remote. So she went back and started all over again, standing in the middle of the drawing--room, eyeing chairs and tables and sofas with a calculating eye. She had her back to the door when Rosie threw it open and called her name.

'If it's coffee,' she said without turning round, 'I'll come now. Rosie, do you suppose the owner would mind if I took Mother's work table?'

It was James who answered her. She spun round to see him standing in the doorway. He said placidly: 'Well, I don't imagine he'd have much use for it, do you?'

Clotilde let out a held breath. Her heart was thundering away so loudly that she was sure that he must hear it. She said in a wooden voice heavy with false calm: 'Good morning—how—unexpected! Will you have some coffee?'

'I'd love some.' He gave her a lazy smile. 'Have you finished your selection or are you just beginning?'

'Just beginning—it's difficult to decide. How—why are you here?'

He gave her a quizzical look. 'Oh, dear, you're looking awfully stern! Shall I go away again?' He contrived to look ill-used and forlorn. 'I had nothing to do and I saw that you had days off, and a run into the country seemed a very good idea.'

Clotilde glanced out of the window; it was going to rain again at any minute and the sky was a lowering hostile grey. 'You really are absurd,' she said, and burst out laughing.

'That's better. You don't do that enough. Where's the coffee?' They went into the hall and he said: 'I do hope you don't mind, but I brought the dogs with me. I thought they might like to meet Tinker.'

They went to the front door and opened it, and there was George, his great head pressed against the window, gazing out, and peering over one shoulder, Millie. They barely stopped to be patted by Clotilde before making a beeline for Tinker, peering cautiously at them from the hall.

'We'll leave the door open,' said Clotilde, 'and they can run around and get to know each other. Did you shut the gate?'

They drank their coffee, ate most of the cake Rosie had baked ready for their tea that afternoon, then called the dogs and went, unheeding of the threatening rain, for a walk. Clotilde, bundled into an old tweed coat, its hood dragged over her hair and quite unconscious of the charming picture she made, threw sticks for the dogs, ran races with them and in between that, carried on an undemanding conversation with James. It was raining quite hard when they turned for home and she said: 'I meant to have finished with the furniture by lunch-time—I've got all the lists to make for Christmas—the ward, you know, presents for the nurses and the patients, and what decorations we're going to have, and extra food and the Boxing Day tea for the relations . . .'

'The mind boggles. Do you know what you want to keep?'

'Yes and no. You see, I ought to choose just a few sensible things so that I can furnish a bedsitter, but there are some quite useless things I'd love to have . . .'

When they reached the house and had taken off their wet things, James said firmly: 'Let's start in here. There's half an hour before lunch, isn't there?'

'It's midday dinner,' said Clotilde. 'Rosie's cooking because she thinks you might be jolly hungry, and there's some sherry left if you'd like some.'

'Rosie is a treasure,' observed James, 'and so are you, Tilly. We'll finish the sherry when we've inspected these rooms downstairs.'

Somehow it made it much easier to choose having James there, not that he said a great deal, only it was always to a good purpose. When they had finished and she read her list, it was to discover that she had an almost equal share of sensible basic furniture and small antique pieces all of which she prized.

'Enough there with which to set up house,' observed James matter-of-factly. 'Presumably you leave it here until you know what to do with it?'

'I don't know—I'd better ask Mr Trent. I'd like to be gone with my bits and pieces before the new owner moves in.'

'And when is that to be?' James asked the question idly.

'Well, that's the point—I don't know. Mr Trent's always so vague and solicitors always take such ages, don't they?'

'Probably everyone's waiting until after Christmas,' said James comfortably.

He went back after tea, making no secret of the fact that he had a dinner date. Clotilde bade him a sedate goodbye, which was perhaps why he merely patted her on the shoulder in an avuncular fashion, remarking carelessly that they would see each other on the ward in a few days' time.

Clotilde was heartily thankful that it was dark enough to hide her disappointment, but indoors, in the kitchen helping Rosie to wash the tea things, her telltale face gave her away.

'He does come and go like,' remarked Rosie, her shrewd eyes on Clotilde's downcast features. 'But there, that's what you'd expect from a friend ... just keeping an eye on you, as it were.'

'Oh, Rosie!' cried Clotilde, and flung down her tea-cloth and flew out of the kitchen and up to her room. She cried hard for five minutes or so, then washed her face and went downstairs again.

Rosie was still in the kitchen, beating eggs for an omelette. 'There isn't any call to fret yourself, love,' she said bracingly. ''E wouldn't have noticed, so cool and calmlike you always are with the doctor.' Then she darted a sharp glance at Clotilde. 'E's a nice man, he'd be that upset . . .'

Clotilde flung her arms round her old friend. 'Oh, Rosie, what a comfort you are! I'd rather die than let him find out.'

'No, dear, there's no call for that, love. But it might be easier if you went away for a while.'

'Yes, I know, and I must. Directly Christmas is over I'll give in my notice and find something miles away— somewhere where I can have a room or a flat. I could still come and see you . . .'

'Of course,' agreed Rosie stoutly. 'I'm free to have visitors if I so wish, the new owner told Mr Trent to tell me that very particular. And later on perhaps Dr Thackery will go somewhere else to work, though if he stays at St Alma's you're not likely to see him even if you got a job at another London hospital.'

'No, but I'd be hoping I would, Rosie, and that wouldn't do.'

She went into the dining room and came back with the rest of the sherry. 'We'll drink to that.' She poured two glasses and tossed her own off, then poured another. Rosie, sipping at her own drink, didn't bat an eyelid when Clotilde poured herself a third glass. She didn't approve of young ladies drinking more than one glass of anything, but in the case of her dear Miss Tilly, she would allow that there had to be an exception to every rule.

Clotilde walked miles the next day, until even Tinker became tired. But it helped, and by the time she was due to go back to London, she had come to terms with herself. It was going to be difficult, but somehow she would have to continue on the same friendly ground she and James had reached. She need not tell him she was leaving; sooner or later he would hear it from someone or other in the hospital, and by then she would have given in her notice and, with luck, have found herself another job. But she wouldn't tell him where she was going. A clean break, and now was the time to make it; she had mastered her sorrow at the loss of her parents, certainly recovered from breaking off her engagement with Bruce, and she had the future in front of her and it was up to her to make something of it. A bit high-flown, she allowed, but she needed to pull her socks up.

Christmas was getting very close. Back at St Alma's Clotilde was caught up in the annual furore of decorations, Christmas trees, presents and the problem of dividing the off duty among her nurses, so that each had a chance of getting away from work for a short time. There was the Hospital Ball too. She had no wish to go, but she would have to put in an appearance. Last year's dress, a gay pink affair, would never do. She browsed around the boutiques in the West End and found a pale grey silk, dusted with silvery stars; it had wide sleeves cuffed at the elbow and a high neckline. She would go for an hour, she decided, and dance with the obligatory partners she was expected to dance with, then she would slip away.

The days rushed past. Going home was out of the question, her free time was fully occupied, making decorations out of crêpe paper, inveigling the sprightliest of her patients into helping. James came on his round, a little austere, she thought, but always pleasant, although he had nothing to say to her other than topics which affected his patients. It was on the morning of the Ball, as he left the ward, flanked by Jeff Saunders and Mary Evans, that he enquired of her if she would be there.

Clotilde told him yes in a quiet voice and wished him a good morning in the same breath. His good morning was equally quiet, but glancing up into his face she had the strong impression that he was amused, although he wasn't smiling and his eyes were half hidden by the heavy lids.

CHAPTER EIGHT

CLOTILDE had elected to be on duty until eight o'clock that evening so that Sally and the student nurses could go off duty at five o'clock and get themselves dolled up ready for the evening. She had help, of course, two nursing aides, both middle-aged and not as quick as she would have liked; but they were pleasant enough and knew what they had to do while she got on with the medicines and treatments and served the suppers. It was half past the hour before she went off duty, and even then she didn't hurry, so that it was almost an hour later by the time she reached the lecture hall where the Ball was being held.

There was no one receiving any more, and she slipped round the edge of the dancers and found a chair between Sister Parsons, due to retire next year, and the hospital chaplain, but she had barely time to do more than say hullo before she was borne off to dance by one of the members of the Hospital Commitee, a rather short stout man who whirled her round and round with tremendous energy and asked her the sort of questions she had come to expect at hospital functions: What did she think of the new E.N.T. Unit? Did she think the lecture hall was better decorated than the previous year, were her nurses happy on the ward and did she realise that the hospital budget was excessive? Economy, boomed her partner in her ear, too much wastage in every department, from kitchen upwards. Clotilde murmured soothingly and presently danced with the hospital secretary, the senior anaesthetist and a consultant surgeon.

She was dancing with Jeff Saunders and wondering if she could slip away as soon as the band stopped when she saw James, head and shoulders above everyone else. His partner was Mary Evans, and Clotilde, without appearing to do so, took in every detail of the girl's dress. Green with a lot of sequins and far too skimpy. The neck was cut far too low; it was meant for an opulent bosom, which Mary Evans most decidedly did not have. I'm growing into a spiteful cat, Clotilde mused, twirling gracefully and listening with every sign of attention to Jeff's description of his small son's first tooth. Presently she allowed herself another look, this time at James. He looked elegant, his dinner jacket, cut by a master hand, no doubt, fitted him to perfection, his shirt dazzling white and finely pleated, put the pastel ruffles and broderie anglaise of some of the younger men there to shame. He looked at her suddenly across the heads of the other dancers and she looked away, her heart thumping. This won't do at all, she thought crossly, I'm behaving like a silly young girl, and the moment the music stopped she said: 'Jeff, I'm going now. It's been lovely, but I've had enough.'

He looked at her with some concern. 'Of course. Shall I come with you?'

She chuckled: 'To the Nurses' Home? That would give everyone something to talk about! I'll slip away.'

'Not before we have had a dance, I hope, Clotilde?' James's voice was gentle in her ear, and Jeff smiled and disappeared into the people milling round them. 'If we don't dance just once,' went on James, 'the grapevine will put it about that we're not on speaking terms, and that would be serious. Appearances must be kept up, don't you agree?'

'Well, all right,' agreed Clotilde, 'but I do want to go . . .'

'And so you shall.' The band had struck up again and he swung her on to the dance floor.

She had danced with him before, of course. Last year it had been a duty dance, a wasted ten minutes while she might have been dancing with Bruce, but now it was different; she wanted the band to play for ever. She made polite conversation—'What a splendid band this year'—and encouraged by his, 'Indeed, yes'—'What pretty dresses the women are wearing!'

'I hadn't noticed. Why are you leaving early?'

She lifted troubled eyes to his. 'I think I didn't want to come in the first place . . .'

'But your parents would have wanted you to enjoy yourself.'

'Yes—Oh, yes. I'm a bit unsettled.'

'Did you have supper before you came? You were late.'

She hadn't thought he had seen her. 'I didn't get off duty until eight o'clock. I forgot about supper. I expect there'll be lashings of food presently.'

'Sandwiches, vol-au-vents, sausage rolls, things in paper cases which slide all over the place, and something unmentionable called cup.'

'The catering department do their best,' she told him.

He danced her to one of the side entrances, opened the door and urged her through it. 'Go and get a coat, or something warm; we'll eat outside.'

Clotilde protested instantly: 'But we can't! I mean, I can leave and no one will notice, but you can't . . .'

Just for one moment his eyes blazed down at her. 'I

do exactly what I please, but if it makes you happier, we'll come back here and join the merrymaking later on. Now run and get that coat.'

She said stubbornly: 'What about Dr Evans?' and watched his eyes blaze once more.

'I wasn't aware that Mary Evans wanted to eat out and she's unlikely to raise any objection—indeed, she's always urging me to eat regular meals.' He added plaintively: 'I missed my lunch.'

'I'll be at the entrance in a few minutes,' said Clotilde, and made for the covered passage connecting the Nurses' Home with the hospital. She felt guilty and excited and reckless, she also felt very hungry.

He took her to Quaglino's and they ate globe artichokes in a piquant sauce, lobster Newburg, mushrooms with chopped truffles and a Waldorf salad, and rounded off these with Ananas Fiona—at least, Clotilde did; James had angels on horseback. They were sitting over their coffee, talking of this and that, when Clotilde glanced at her watch. She was just a bit hazy, what with a champagne cocktail and two glasses of hock, and she blinked and looked again. 'Look at the time!' she gasped. 'The Ball will be over. My goodness—we must go!'

James studied her pretty face. 'We shall be back just nicely in time for the last dance.'

'But I wasn't going back . . .'

'In that case, we can stay here,' and when she protested: 'Better still, we'll dance in the entrance hall, just the two of us.'

She wasn't sure if he was serious. She said quickly: 'We can't do that,' and when he smiled at her she was sure he had been joking. All the same, she said: 'I really think I should go back . . .'

Illogically, she was quite disappointed when he agreed without demur. On their way he asked her: 'Do you get any time off at Christmas? Katrina wants you to spend the day with her—not Christmas Day, of course, she knows that's impossible, but Boxing Day or the day after that, perhaps?'

'How kind of her, but I can't—you see, the nurses on the ward have all got their plans laid; they each get a day off in turn. As Rosie's going to stay with her niece, I arranged to be on duty. I—I really don't mind.'

Afraid he would argue about it, she went on brightly: 'Thank you for my dinner, it was heavenly,' and then, anxiously: 'Shall we be back in time? You'll have been missed.'

'I'm flattered. Katrina's going to be disappointed. Perhaps we can arrange something for Old Year's Night. Here we are and the band's still playing. How about the dance?'

Something she would have liked more than anything in the world. 'No—no, thank you. It's been lovely, but I really must . . .' She sought feverishly for excuses as they went through the door. 'I can't—oh, I can't,' she mumbled, and turned and flew away, down the passage to the Nurses' Home, up the staircase and into her room. She could still hear the band faintly. James would be there by now, probably dancing with Mary Evans. She tried to remember who else he had danced with during the evening; most of his partners had been wives of other consultants and members of the committee; he'd danced with Sally and Jo and several of the other sisters, but he hadn't singled any one of them out, only Mary Evans; he'd danced with her at least twice. He would be with her now, probably explaining in his calm way that he had taken Sister Collins out for a meal because she had needed cheering up.

Clotilde wept while she undressed and went on weeping once she was in her bed. Finally she slept, but she felt terrible the next morning, but then so did almost everyone else. The dance had gone on until three o'clock and they hadn't had enough sleep.

There was time, between the feverish preparations for Christmas, to visit Mr Trent once again. He studied the list of furniture she handed him, pronounced her choice to be a most sensible one and informed her that the new owner intended to take up residence in the New Year. 'Although I believe,' observed Mr Trent in his dry old voice, 'that that largely depends on circumstances. I understand that—er—Rosie will be staying with her niece over the holiday period. Will you be going down to Wendens Ambo before Christmas?'

'Yes, the weekend before. I've got a few clothes still there, I'll pack them up and bring them back with me. I don't think I'll go again. I've been very lucky being able to go there so often now that it's not my home any more.'

'Indeed yes. You have plans now? Definite plans?'

'Oh, yes. I shall give in my notice tomorrow. I've seen several jobs that might do . . .'

'In London?'

'No, there's a post in Birmingham, and another in Liverpool and one in Edinburgh, but I'm not sure about that one, it's a bit far away from Rosie.' She smiled a little. 'She's all I've got.'

'Of course. Well, I must wish you a happy future, Clotilde.' Mr Trent coughed. 'I suppose you never hear from that young doctor to whom you were engaged? You have no wish to find work near him?'

'Good lord, no—I never think of him now and I don't mind if I never see him again.'

It could almost be said that Mr Trent smirked. 'Just as well, Clotilde, just as well.' He added: 'There are as good fish in the sea as ever came out of it.'

Clotilde agreed with him, only she wasn't lucky enough to catch her particular fish.

She went back on duty, puzzled over the off duty list and nursed her patients to a very high standard of care, and the next morning went to the office and gave in her notice. The Principal Nursing Officer, a stern lady who never showed emotion, allowed the severity of her features to relax a little. 'I'm not altogether surprised,' she observed to Clotilde. 'You've had rather more than your share of hard knocks during the last month or so, perhaps a complete change will benefit you. I shall be sorry to see you go, of course, you're a competent and intelligent young woman, and they're rather thin on the ground. Have you any ideas as to your future?'

Clotilde told her about Birmingham and Liverpool, and added: 'I was wondering if I would go abroad.'

'I should look around first,' advised her companion, and went on rather severely: 'Running away isn't much help, Sister Collins.'

Clotilde mumbled meekly. There was no point in disagreeing with Miss Scott, who was self-opinionated and middle-aged. She would do exactly what she liked, thought Clotilde grumpily, and it would depend if she felt like going to some outlandish spot; if she did she would go. In the meantime she said all the right things and got herself out of the office.

The remainder of the week was taken up with preparations for Christmas; as many patients as were able to were to go home, some happily discharged,

some to return in three or four days' time. There were
several ill women to whom Christmas would mean very
little, and these Clotilde moved to the end of the ward.
It was more awkward for the nurses to keep an eye on
them, but on the other hand they would enjoy what
peace and quiet there was, away from the tree and the
decorations and visitors. She spent her off duty
shopping for the patients, choosing presents for the
nurses and laying in a stock of nuts and chocolates and
potato crisps. Sherry she already had—James had sent
half a dozen bottles with his compliments; she stocked
up in soft drinks and beer, made sure there was coffee
and tea in plenty and spent long hours tying up parcels
and labelling them. Even with help from the nurses, it
took up a good deal of her time.

James did a round the day before she intended going
home. He took longer than usual, pondering each case
so that everyone who could possibly go home should
have the chance to do so. Clotilde had provided him
with a list of her patients who had no family and who
lived alone, and with the utmost tactfulness, he pointed
out to each of them in turn that they were really not
quite fit enough to go home and would they mind
staying over Christmas. The relief on their faces was
pathetic..

The round over, coffee, with the addition of mince
pies in honour of the festive season, was served in
Clotilde's office. She hadn't seen James to speak to
since the night of the Ball and she avoided him now,
presenting a professional front hard to crack. She
listened to Mary Evans gushing about the party the
medical staff were giving that evening and to which
James had been invited. It was, according to her, going
to be an all-night affair. She was at some pains to tell

Clotilde this and remarked laughingly: 'Aren't you envious, Sister Collins? You must find life very dull now that Bruce has gone.' And just by way of piling it on: 'I hear he's dating one of the medical students—her father's a grocer with lashings of money.'

To all of which Clotilde said nothing, just smiled calmly and nodded and observed that the party sounded fun and she hoped everyone would enjoy themselves. James, taking the chance to talk to Jeff, hadn't even turned his head, but she was sure he had heard every word. Would he have been surprised, she wondered silently, if she had leaned across the desk and pulled Mary Evans' hair and boxed her ears?

She bade them all a dignified goodbye at the ward door and went back to her office, where she sat, fighting for calm, until Sally came to tell her that dinners were ready to be served.

The nurses, looking at her white strained face, muttered to each other that she looked pretty ghastly, and because they liked her, went out of their way to be helpful. Clotilde, silently slightly bewildered by their earnest responses to her directions, observed to Sally that it must be the Christmas spirit got into them all. 'They're always pretty good, but they're positively motherly!'

And Sally, although she made a laughing remark, quite understood why. Clotilde, usually so serene and content with her lot, looked so pale and pinched that someone must have upset her badly. Not Dr Thackery, surely? Sally had been harbouring hopeful ideas about Clotilde and him ever since Bruce had left, but it seemed that they were to come to nothing. Mary Evans had looked like the cat that had got at the cream as they had left the office. She must have said something, or hinted at something. There had been a good deal of joking about her and her efforts to attract Dr Thackery's attention, but no one had seriously thought they would come to anything.

Clotilde had two days off on the following morning and she was going home that evening. Before she went she told Sally that she had given in her notice. 'But don't tell anyone, I've only told you so that you can apply for my job. I'm pretty sure you'll get it.' She had waited until the last minute before giving her news, and didn't stop to hear more than Sally's startled: 'Sister Collins . . .'

'We'll talk about it when I get back.'

It was a very wet, very cold night when she left the hospital and the roads were treacherous with frost. She drove carefully and arrived home to find Rosie waiting for her with hot soup and mince pies and a bottle of sherry the Vicar had given her.

They sat up late, drinking half the sherry and then making a pot of tea while Tinker dozed in front of the stove. He was to stay with Rosie; it seemed that the new owner had no objection to him remaining—indeed, Mr Trent had written to say that he would be a useful guard dog for Rosie when she was on her own. 'He'll miss you, Miss Tilly, but you will come and see us as often as you can?'

'Of course!' Clotilde made her voice cheerfully brisk. 'If I take the Birmingham job I can drive over on my days off quite easily. After all, since Mother and Father died, he's got used to being here with you. He won't be too much for you, Rosie?'

'Lor', no Miss Tilly! He's good company of an evening.' She poured more tea for them both. 'So you've given in your notice. You'll come again before you leave?' She sounded so anxious that Clotilde hastened to reassure her.

'Of course, my next free days after Christmas—after that, we'll see. I don't know when the new owner's coming, do you?'

Rosie shook her head. 'A very easy gent he must be. Generous too—he could have given me notice any time, instead of which, here I am, as snug as can be, and you, Miss Tilly, with the chance of coming back now and again.'

Clotilde agreed a little doubtfully; perhaps it would have been better if she had cut loose completely. Perhaps, in time, when she had got used to her new life, she would be able to do that.

She spent the next day walking with Tinker in the blustery weather, loving the feel of the cold wind on her face and the crunch of frost under her boots, and the following day, before she went back to the hospital, she packed Rosie and Tinker into the car, and drove them to her niece's house. It was a wrench leaving them there, and Rosie wept as she pressed two beribboned parcels into her hands. 'One from me and one from Tinker,' she explained, and, 'Oh, Miss Tilly, I do hope that next Christmas we'll be together again. I do try to be cheerful, but things 'ave gone a bit against us, haven't they?'

Clotilde gave her a great hug. 'Dear Rosie, it'll blow over—things do. By next Christmas I'll have a nice little home going and we'll spend Christmas together—Tinker too, of course.'

She bent to hug the dog too, then got into the car.

'You'll go straight back to the hospital?' asked Rosie, anxiously.

'Yes, dear. And I'll phone you on Christmas Day. Have a nice time with everyone.'

She drove off quickly, not looking back. It was still

early evening. She turned the Mini towards Wendens Ambo; just one last look, she promised herself, and when she got there, got out of the car and went into the house, to walk slowly through it. After Christmas it wouldn't be hers any longer; she would come from time to time, but only as a visitor to Rosie. She thought it might be very much better if she stayed away altogether, but then Rosie would be upset. She locked the door and got into the Mini again and drove slowly back to the hospital. In three days' time it would be Christmas and there was plenty to keep her busy until then.

Dr Evans was early on the ward the next morning, making her round just as the nurses were getting patients up and making beds; the very worst time. She was in a bad mood too, demanding this and that to be done. All the same, Clotilde saw that she had all she needed and then politely asked her if she would like coffee. To her surprise, she agreed, and Clotilde led the way to the office, wondering what on earth they would talk about. Sally brought in the tray and Clotilde told her to fetch a mug and have coffee with them. The ward was quiet, running on the oiled wheels Clotilde had so painstakingly instigated, and conversation would be easier with the three of them.

Christmas was a safe topic, of course, but Dr Evans quickly introduced a more personal note. 'The party was tremendous fun,' she said chattily. 'It went on for hours—James was the most marvellous companion.' She shot a look at Clotilde, who remained poker-faced and said amiably: 'I'm glad it was such a success.'

'Well, we had to celebrate. I've not told anyone yet, of course, but he's as thrilled as I am.' She gave a girlish giggle that made Clotilde wince. 'And don't ask me to let you into the secret!'

'All right, I won't, Dr Evans. Did you enjoy the Ball?'

Mary Evans looked disconcerted, but there was nothing in Clotilde's quiet face to give a hint as to her feelings. 'Oh, yes, it wasn't too bad—too many people there, though, and some of the men seemed to think it was a good chance to go off and consult together. James was gone for hours. I told him off when he got back, and all he said was that he'd taken the opportunity to deal with an unexpected problem.'

Clotilde murmured politely. The unexpected problem, of course, was James's need for a good square meal. She offered more coffee, assured Dr Evans that she would be on duty over Christmas, and walked down the ward with her. She then went back to the office where Sally was stacking the mugs.

'Get another pot of coffee,' she begged. 'I'll send two of the nurses to their coffee break, the other two can take round the drinks.' And when Sally had come back with a full coffee pot. 'That girl—how tiresome she is!'

'She's ghastly—and all that talk about Dr Thackery and their secret. Do you suppose they are engaged? She's been cocky enough these last few days. If they are, he's concealing his feelings beautifully. And I bet she doesn't call him James to his face.'

'Well, if they're engaged she does.' Clotilde spoke cheerfully, for if the truth were told she was so numb with shock and surprise that at the moment, at any rate, she felt nothing. She found it hard to believe, but it was more than likely to be true; Katrina had said someone at the hospital, hadn't she, and Mary Evans had been throwing out hints for some time now, and this morning had been rather more than a hint.

Clotilde looked into her coffee cup and sighed

soundlessly. She had never had a chance with James, she would have to get him out of her system as soon as possible and in the meanwhile preserve a friendly front so that he would never suspect.

She drank the rest of her coffee. 'It's round day tomorrow—I wonder what sort of hair-do she'll have? Let's get cracking, shall we? We're so slack I'll take the two juniors for a teaching round if you'll get Mrs Dove to X-Ray and send someone down to the Dispensary about that Lasix—it's in the book, but there's no sign of it.'

The full force of Mary Evans' remark didn't strike her until the end of the day as she was going off duty, when she caught sight of James leaving the hospital with Dr Evans beside him. She stopped at a window to watch them get into the Bentley and drive away.

She went to her room and washed her hair, then changed and presently went down to supper, where she was the life and soul of the party.

She hardly slept a wink, and to get up in the morning was a relief.

Since it was round day there was plenty of work to keep her busy. Besides, the post had swollen out of all proportion with an influx of Christmas cards, so that the distribution of them took her a lot longer than usual. Two porters had put up a tree in the centre of the ward, too, and once Dr Thackery had gone, everyone with a few minutes to spare would be decorating it. There were paper chains to be put up too and the wreaths of paper flowers they had all been busy with in their spare moments. She was only just ready when the doors opened and James came in, with Jeff beside him and Mary Evans trying to get between them. His 'Good morning, Sister,' was exactly as usual, but he went on briskly: 'We'll be as quick as we can today. I'm sure Sister has a great deal to do, and most fortunately, none of our patients are in need of intensive treatment.' He glanced at Clotilde. 'You are taking emergencies, though?'

'Yes, sir. There are four empty beds and both side wards empty.'

'Well, let's hope they won't be filled. Now let's look at Mrs Dove . . .'

The round ran its course, interlarded by pleasant little seasonal jokes and the exchange of greetings between the doctor and his patients, and when they reached the office there was a handsome beribboned box of chocolates and two bottles of the finest sherry on Clotilde's desk, James's annual gift to her and the nurses on the ward. She thanked him pleasantly, poured coffee and joined in the desultory talk while they drank it. Beyond a few changed pills and drugs, his instructions had been few and there was no need to discuss any of the patients. 'We shall pay for this peace and quiet,' observed James as he got up to go, 'we always do.'

At the ward door he paused. 'I shall be here to carve the turkey, Sister. Good day to you.'

She bade him good morning, smiled at his companions and went back into the ward. All she wanted to do was to find somewhere quiet where she could sit and cry her eyes out in peace, but since that was impossible she pinned a smile on her face and suggested that since there was half an hour before dinners would be brought to the ward, they might as well start decorating the tree.

By the time she went off duty that evening the ward was transformed, paper flowers, some of them a highly

improbable colour, hung in great bunches from the
ceiling, wreaths hung over every bed and paper chains
criss-crossed the ward. The tree, topped by a fairy
doll and festooned with tinsel, dominated the place,
its coloured lights switched on. Clotilde, doing her
evening round before she went off duty and listening
to the pleased remarks of her patients, forgot how
tired she was. If it made a lot of extra work and all
had to be cleared away in three days' time, it was still
worth the trouble just to see the pleasure on their
faces. And tomorrow—Christmas Eve—she would
have to arrange the packages round the tree at the
last possible minute. She would be on duty until eight
o'clock; she would go to supper and then come back
and do that when lights were out; the night nurses
could help her.

Two of the student nurses had days off for
Christmas. Sally had a half day on Christmas Eve so
that she could spend it with her boy-friend, which left
Clotilde with only two nurses, but the ward wasn't
busy, so she had given them both the morning off and
she herself wouldn't be going off duty. The day's work
went easily enough, although she was glad enough when
the night staff took over and she could go to supper.
She didn't hurry over the meal; most of her friends were
there, grumbling cheerfully about the other extra tasks
and overtime they were doing and making plans for the
additional free time they would have once everything
was normal again. They got up to go presently and she
promised to join them in the Sisters' sitting room once
she had been back to the ward.

The night nurses, anxious to have a quiet night, had
worked hard; another ten minutes or so and they were
ready for the lights to be put out, and Clotilde was able

to go down the ward with them and arrange the gaily covered presents round the tree. Not all the patients were asleep, but beyond a whispered goodnight, they didn't say anything. Clotilde thanked the nurses and slipped quietly out of the ward.

The sitting room was almost full. Nearly everyone had been on duty all day and they certainly would be all the next day too; their own pleasures would have to wait until after Christmas, but there was a cake on the side table, and a dish of nuts and crisps and a plate of sausage rolls flanked by a bottle of sherry. Clotilde cast off her cap and sat down on the end of one of the sofas. Presently they would exchange small gifts and have a drink and then go to bed, although probably someone would make a pot of tea and they'd sit around talking in someone's room. She would miss their companionship, she thought, looking round at the faces of her friends.

The door opened and Sister Adams, elderly, disapproving and in a hurry to get to her bed, put her head round the door. 'Sister Collins, you're wanted at the entrance.'

'Me?' asked Clotilde, and reached for her cap. 'Are you sure?'

'Of course I'm sure. What silly questions you young women ask!' snapped Sister Adams, and withdrew her head.

Clotilde, sticking pins back into her cap, frowned. 'Who on earth can it be at this hour? I bet it's a relation with a parcel for one of the patients. Leave me some sherry.'

James was in the entrance hall. Clotilde slithered to a halt and said: 'Oh,' then looked around to see if there was anyone else there.

'There you are', observed James mildly. 'Your cap's on crooked. I've brought Katrina to see you.'

'Oh,' said Clotilde again, and twitched her cap straight with a peevish hand while she stared at him. He was wearing a dinner jacket with a beautifully tailored coat open over it. He looked distinguished and handsome, he also looked amused.

'Had a busy day?' he wanted to know. 'The car's outside.'

'Where's Katrina?' She sounded so suspicious that he laughed outright.

'In the car, of course.' He held the door open for her, then popped her into the Bentley and got in himself.

Katrina was sitting in the back, looking as lovely as Clotilde would have liked to have looked and smelling delicious. She gave a pleased squeal as Clotilde sat down. 'Hullo, Tilly. Did you think I'd forgotten you? Well, I haven't. I do wish you could spend Christmas with us at home, but James has promised me he'll drive you down for New Year. Won't that be fun? I don't go back to Leyden until the middle of January and we'll have a day out shopping too before then.' She paused for breath. 'I've brought you a present.' She pressed a large package into Clotilde's hands. 'I do hope you'll like it. Open it, do!'

Clotilde said weakly: 'Oh, how kind you are. Of course I'll open it.' And she undid the soft ribbon round it. It was a Gucci bag, brown calf, expensively simple and quite exquisite. Clotilde drew a deep breath. 'Oh, I say,' she began. 'It's simply gorgeous—what a heavenly present!'

'Oh, good—you like it. That's a lovely scarf you sent me, Tilly—thanks a lot. I do love Christmas—all the presents and parties. James, is there time to take Tilly for a drink somewhere?'

Clotilde said too quickly: 'Thank you, but I must get back; there's still quite a bit to do.' She eyed Katrina's green taffeta dress with appreciative eyes. 'You look lovely, Katrina.'

'Actually,' said Katrina slowly, 'you look rather fetching yourself in that funny little cap and that uniform, doesn't she, James?'

He was lounging in the front seat, not saying anything much. 'The Sisters' uniform at St Alma's is very attractive,' he said blandly.

Clotilde carefully folded the ribbons and put the handbag back into its box. 'It was sweet of you to come,' she said addressing Katrina. 'I hope that you—all of you—have a wonderful Christmas.' She leaned forward and kissed Katrina's cheek. 'I really must go.'

James got out of the car without demur, opened the door and went the few yards with her to the entrance. He went inside with her and stood looking down at her. 'What did I give you last year?' he asked her.

'A leather notecase,' she said promptly.

'And the year before that it was a leather wallet, wasn't it? And this year, nothing, Tilly, and do you know why? I'm unable to give you what I wish, and I have no present for you . . .'

She said chattily to hide her sudden hurt: 'Oh, that doesn't matter—finding Christmas presents is a lengthy business, isn't it? Besides, you've given us those luscious chocolates and the sherry.'

She didn't want to stand there talking to no purpose. She said firmly: 'I really must go. It was lovely seeing Katrina. Goodnight.'

She went back to the sitting room and the handbag went from one to the other and was duly admired. 'Nice to have rich friends,' said someone cheerfully. 'How about tea if all the sherry's finished?'

They went to bed eventually, still laughing and talking and opening presents. Clotilde took another look at the handbag and put it in a drawer. How like Katrina, she thought fondly, to buy an extravagant present like that. She might be spoilt, but she was sweet-natured with it.

It was snowing, most appropriately, when they went on duty the next morning. Clotilde listened to the night report, handed out her presents to the nurses, received hers in turn and sent the night staff off duty so that they could get into their beds and get up early if they wished. Then she sailed into the ward where to the sound of Christmas music over the hospital radio, she did her round and then joined the nurses in making beds and getting up those ladies who were capable of sitting around. No one went to coffee; they drank it in her office in turn, two at a time, and ate the mince pies she had provided before doing a quick round once more to make sure that every patient was looking her best.

James arrived on the stroke of twelve o'clock, nicely timed to meet the trolley bearing the turkey being wheeled into the ward from the kitchen. But first he went round the ward too, with Mary Evans trailing him closely and Clotilde in attendance.

He had wished her a happy Christmas on his arrival and she had replied suitably. Jeff had given her a kiss, Mary Evans had said nothing at all, and two of the students, who had been coerced into giving a hand, took the opportunity of kissing her too, watched by James with a bland face.

'And now to work?' he enquired, and the silkiness of his voice sent them at once to the trolley.

He carved as he appeared to do everything else, with an easy competence. Clotilde, dishing vegetables, directed the handing out of the plates while one student filled glasses with the lemonade the doctor had decreed should take the place of anything stronger. And by the time the remains of the turkey had been wheeled away, and the plates collected, Clotilde had gone to the kitchen to see about the Christmas pudding. With everything in readiness she issued the annual invitation to her helpers to have a drink and ushered them into the office, leaving Sally to supervise the last of the clearing up and feeding which had to be done.

James had never stayed long at these obligatory functions; he drank his sherry, thanked everyone with charming politeness and begged to be excused. Mary Evans begged to be excused too, and Clotilde, listening to one of the students, didn't see the faint surprise on James's face. She had taken a quick look at Mary's left hand when the party had arrived, but there was no ring on it. Perhaps they were going off to spend Christmas together somewhere and James would give her the ring then. She went quite pale at the thought, so that the student wanted to know if she felt all right.

The rest of them put down their glasses and went with James, and Clotilde went down the ward with them, a little behind the rest, because Jeff, who was the one on duty, wanted to tell her something about one of the patients. James had stopped to speak to each nurse in turn and at the door thanked her again, before wishing her, in his most placid manner, a pleasant time for the rest of the Christmas period.

Clotilde watched him walk rapidly away, with the rest of them trying to keep up. A pleasant time, indeed! she thought indignantly; as if being on duty for the rest of the day, dealing with the small upsets her patients were bound to have, supervising visitors teas, entertaining anyone who chose to visit the ward, rearranging the ward on Boxing Day ready for the students' concert and clearing up the decorations and mess afterwards, meant she was going to have a very pleasant time. Feeling very ill done by, she went to see her charges and then, smiling and ready with a word for everyone, pulled crackers with all but the most timid of her patients.

The nurses ate their lunch in the office; sausage rolls, sandwiches and more mince pies sent up from the kitchens, and then, while there was a quiet spell during the afternoon and the patients' rest period, she sent them two by two to wander round the hospital, to inspect the other wards, meet their friends and eat and drink anything they were offered. Indeed it was so quiet that presently she sent Sally off to try and find her current boy-friend, one of the students attached to the Senior Surgical Consultant. 'As long as you're back by three o'clock,' she reminded her. 'There's nothing in theatre, is there? He may be free then.'

After Sally had gone she went round the ward once more; her patients slept, each and every one of them. She went back to the office and sat down at her desk and allowed her thoughts to dwell on James. Sitting in his lovely house with Mary Evans, no doubt, or perhaps he had driven down to his parents' home. And what about Katrina? She was trying to arrange things logically when she heard the ward door swing open and hurried out silently, her finger to her lips, anxious for her patients.

It was James, laughing silently at her as he came, equally silently, to meet her. He took her arm and turned her round and back into the office, leaving the door open.

'An admission?' she asked. 'I thought Jeff was on call.'

'He is. As far as I know there are no admissions—you'll get those tomorrow as we always do. You looked so fierce this morning, I was almost afraid to speak to you, Tilly.'

He was standing very close to her so that she had to lean back a bit to look into his face. 'How ridiculous! I wasn't in the least fierce—I've really had rather a busy time . . .'

'Oh, was that it? In that case, I can do as Katrina bade me without having my ears boxed.' He bent swiftly and kissed her long and hard. 'Do you know what that is?' he asked her.

Clotilde took a steadying breath and did her best to be normal, which was difficult in the circumstances. 'No,' she managed.

'That's my farewell salute to Sister Clotilde Collins.' He grinned at her. 'You can think about that until I see you again, Tilly.'

He had gone—just like that, leaving her wanting to shout a dozen questions at him. Did he know she was leaving? Probably the Principal Nursing Officer had told him, or was it an oblique way of letting her know that he was going to get married to that awful Mary Evans? She could have screamed with annoyance. And why had he come back? Or perhaps he hadn't left the hospital; Men's Medical would have had Dr Fox, the Second Senior Consultant, to carve their turkey; they would have met for a drink in the consultants' room. Clotilde went and looked out of the window, just in time to see the Bentley turning out of the gates at the end of the courtyard. Most annoyingly, she couldn't see if there was anyone with him.

CHAPTER NINE

SOMEHOW or other, Clotilde got through the rest of Christmas, presenting a cheerful face to the small world of hospital, lending a sympathetic ear to the mild dissatisfactions of her patients, going to infinite trouble to keep them happy. Then listening to endless relations wanting to know what exactly was wrong with Mother or Aunty or Granny, entertaining visitors; important dignitaries, innumerable students, her friends when they could leave their wards for ten minutes, and on the day after Boxing Day they began the task of getting everything back to normal as quickly as possible.

The night staff helped. Once the patients had settled for the night they crept round the ward, stealthily collecting paper chains and anything else they could reach easily, so that when Clotilde came on duty in the morning it only remained for the chains and wreaths to be dismantled. The ward looked very bare, but it made their work easier. Besides, it was the consultant's round that morning and Clotilde was aware that the doctors, while entering willingly enough into the Christmas spirit, liked all trace of it away the moment Christmas was over; none of that Twelfth Night business for them. So that by the time James was due to arrive, the ward was back to pristine orderliness. The empty beds had been filled, of course, but that was to be expected. It was a pity that this time their new occupants were all elderly, and because they bore a grudge against Fate allowing them to fall ill at a time when they were all set to enjoy themselves, they were both gloomy and peevish. Clotilde led the way to the first of them and watched with admiration while James charmed her into a better frame of mind.

'Home in no time,' he assured her. 'We'll soon have that chest as good as new—in the meantime make the most of the rest here, you'll enjoy yourself all the more when you get home again.' He left her actually smiling and passed on to the next patient. Undoubtedly he had a splendid bedside manner, thought Clotilde as she led the way to an old lady who had been in the ward for some time now, and whom he greeted like an old friend.

The round went well. Even the ill patients had improved, although for two of them it would only be a temporary improvement, brought about by the euphoria of the last few days. James stayed to talk to them with kindly gentleness after he had finished examining them, giving them his unhurried attention. In Clotilde's office presently he observed: 'Both Mrs Twist and Mrs White are failing fast, aren't they, Sister? We'd better increase ... let me see, how much are they getting now?'

He looked at Jeff, but Dr Evans answered, adding a few details importantly. James didn't look up, merely went on writing on the charts and then handing them to Clotilde. His smile was brief and friendly and she smiled in return, pleasantly cool and quite impersonal, delighted that she had herself so well in hand, to have that coolness shattered by his: 'Perhaps you will rearrange your off duty, Sister. Katrina expects you for Old Year's Night.'

Her heart bounced. 'I'm afraid that's quite impossible, Sir—I've already made out the off duty ...'

He glanced at Sally, who had come in with the coffee, and she said at once: 'I'll change with you,

Sister. As a matter of fact I'd rather have your days off than mine.'

'That's settled, then,' said James in the placid no-nonsense voice Clotilde always found so hard to ignore. 'I'll pick you up about seven o'clock. You'll stay the night, of course.'

Clotilde sought for words. She was furious at his high-handed arrangements, she was also giddy with delight and at the same time apprehensive of Mary Evans' reactions. Perhaps she would be going too. Clotilde stole a look at her, and although she looked angry she was silent. That would be it, then. She was to go with the pair of them to Shaftesbury, not because James particularly wanted her company, but because his spoilt young sister wanted to see her again. Probably both he and Mary were annoyed at her having to be there, playing gooseberry. She turned an impassive face upon her staff nurse. 'Thank you, Sally, in that case we'll do as you suggest and change duties.' She began to pour the coffee, trying not to listen to the lighthearted conversation James had started with Mary Evans, while she pondered the chances of him getting to hear that she was leaving before she wanted him to. She would tell him, of course, but only at the last minute. Secrets, however well kept, had a nasty way of escaping, and it would be all over St Alma's in no time at all. She could safely leave it for another week, and by then she would have had replies from Birmingham and Bristol. It would be much easier to confront him with the news that she had a job waiting for her.

James made no mention of Katrina's invitation; he bade her good morning with only the faintest of smiles, apparently oblivious of Mary Evans' vindictive stare at Clotilde. Jeff was the only one who was the same as usual, with his cheeful: 'See you tomorrow, Tilly.'

Clotilde spent the next two days wondering how she could get out of going with James, and on the third morning there he was again to do another round and she no clearer as to what she should do. The temptation to go to his parents' home was very great. On the other hand, much as she disliked Mary Evans, it seemed very unfair on the girl to foist her company on the pair of them. She went on duty with her mind made up. She wasn't going.

The round, for some reason, took a good deal longer than usual, and coffee was drunk in a businesslike fashion, while those cases which needed to be discussed were. Clotilde's firm: 'I should like a word with you, Dr Thackery,' was met by an equally firm: 'Not now, Clotilde,' and he was up and away before she could get to the door. Considerably nettled by this deviation from hospital manners, Clotilde swished back to the office. Sally was there, sorting charts, putting the papers James had scattered all over the desk back into order.

'Well, she could have said goodbye!' she declared as Clotilde sat down.

'Who?'

'Why, our Mary, Sister. Off to Cardiff this evening—got herself a house surgeon's post there. All done in quite a hurry too. I suppose she came to the conclusion that there was no future with Dr Thackery—matrimonially-wise, that is. That's why it's all a bit hush-hush, I daresay. After all, she was pretty obvious about her crush on him, wasn't she?' She broke off to ask: 'Are you feeling okay, Sister? You're awfully pale.'

'I'm fine—just tired. I didn't know about Dr Evans.' Clotilde added reluctantly: 'Actually I thought she and Dr Thackery were serious about each other ...'

Sally chuckled. 'She may have been, but anyone could see with half an eye that she wasn't his sort.'

Clotilde said incoherently: 'I thought—that is, his sister told me ... and I imagined it to be Dr Evans. I ...' She stopped and drew a sharp breath and began again. 'We'd better get these forms down to X-Ray.'

Sally took her lead at once. 'And shall I get Mrs Trevor up now, or wait until after the rest hour?'

They plunged into the day-to-day planning of the ward work, and presently went to serve the dinners. Dr Evans wasn't mentioned again. That didn't mean to say that Clotilde didn't think about her a great deal. Had she refused James? she wondered. Had he ever proposed? And if not, who had Katrina been talking about? Doing her evening round, she stopped short by Mrs Trevor, sitting grumpily in a chair. James had said something very strange—about saying goodbye to Sister Collins, or some such nonsense, surely he hadn't meant...? No wishful thinking, she told herself bracingly; just because she was head over heels in love with him, she had no reason to be fanciful. She heard Mrs Trevor's complaining voice, going on and on and cut it short with a soothing: 'Well, we'll pop you back into bed, Mrs Trevor,' and moved on to exchange a meaningless conversation with the next patient. Linda Bond was in the bed at the end of the ward by the door; seventeen years old, a pert, pretty little Cockney, she was recovering nicely from pneumonia. She invited Clotilde to admire the clothes in the fashion magazine she was reading and observed cheekily: 'Yer could do with a bit of smartenin' up, Sister. Proper down in the dumps you are. Yer can't be all that old.' She winked and nodded. 'Got a boy-friend, have yer? If yer 'aven't, it's time yer did.'

The door opened as she spoke and James walked in. 'E'd do nicely,' said Linda.

'I'm glad to hear it,' observed James equably. 'Sister, you wanted to speak to me?'

'Yes, no—I don't know ...' Clotilde, her calm in tatters, went pink in the face, and added even more obscurely: 'It doesn't matter.'

'Perhaps you were going to tell me you're leaving?' His placid voice held no curiosity.

'Cor, getting married, are yer?' asked the incorrigible Linda. 'Well, it ain't right for yer to be stuck 'ere in that silly cap all yer life. S'right, ain't it, Doctor?'

'Quite right, Linda, though I don't agree about the cap. I rather like it.'

'Did you want to see someone?' asked Clotilde severely.

He smiled slowly at her. 'In the office, I think, Sister.'

He gave Linda another smile, a quite different one, though, and walked with Clotilde down the ward and into the office. Once there, he said placidly: 'Sit down, Tilly,' and shut the door and leant against it. 'Now tell me ...'

But now that she had the chance she couldn't find the words. She mumbled: 'You know I'm leaving.'

'Oh yes. Did you really think you could keep it a secret? What are your plans?'

She stared at the plain silk tie he was wearing. He wore nice ties. She said, still mumbling: 'There's a job in Birmingham and another one at the Bristol Royal Infirmary.'

'But you've not decided?'

'No.'

'Good. Now I'm going to talk, and you're not going to interrupt.'

He left the door and came to sit on the edge of her desk, looming over her. 'Let's just put several things right. I've been very diverted from time to time to hear rumours about myself and Mary Evans—so absurd that I never gave them a second thought. But upon reflection, I believe you did?' He paused waiting for her to speak, so she said, 'Yes,' without looking at him. 'You know now that they're pure fantasy, they can be forgotten. They're of no importance.' He bent over and picked up one of her hands and held it between his. 'You agree?'

'Yes,' said Clotilde, and thought how very comforting his hands felt.

'Another matter entirely,' went on James in his calm way. 'Your home—I'm the new owner.'

Her eyes flew to his face. 'You? Why? And you didn't tell me . . .'

'It seemed the logical thing to do. Mr Trent agreed with me; so did Rosie.'

'But you didn't tell me,' said Clotilde crossly. 'Why not?'

'At the time the circumstances weren't in my favour.'

'So why are they now?' she snapped, quite put out.

'That, my darling, is what I am about to tell you.' James gave a great sigh as the phone rang and he lifted the receiver, and Clotilde, her face glowing from the 'darling', watched as he listened.

She would have to wait to hear whatever it was he was going to tell her; she saw his face grow remote and thoughtful and heard his brief answers. He put down the phone presently, all trace of his former manner gone.

'There's an outbreak of food poisoning—a wedding party in Tutty Street, about thirty, they think. How many beds have we?'

'Four, and two in the side wards, and I can put up six down the centre.'

'Good—arrange that, will you? Let's hope they won't be needed, but let's be ready. I'll go down to the Accident Room and see if there's anything to be admitted. Ring Jeff to join me there, will you? Oh, and my new houseman—his name is Pratt. Get him too.'

He went to the door and then back he came to where Clotilde was already lifting the phone. 'We can wait, they can't,' he said softly, and kissed her.

Clotilde allowed herself half a minute of pure happiness and then went into action. The phoning done, she collected the two nurses and the nursing aide who were on duty, set them to getting the empty beds ready, then went back to the phone to ask for more beds. She was leaving the office when the phone rang to say that two patients were on their way up and there would be at least six more. 'They're still coming in,' said the voice, 'so expect more than that.'

The first two were in a bad way, already dehydrated and in a good deal of pain. Clotilde, setting up drips, directing bowls and clean linen, undressing the sufferers, still in their wedding finery, was hardly aware of James. She did as he asked with the efficiency of long practice, had more beds made up, gave the drugs he ordered, and in between whiles, showed poor young Mr Pratt, pitched in at the deep end with a vengeance, where the essential ward equipment was. Jeff joined them presently, coming up from the Accident Room with the news that there were two more women to admit, both rather ill.

'I've had two beds put up in the side wards,' said Clotilde. 'It'll be crowded, but it's the best that I can do.'

'Thank God it's only a matter of a day or two before they're better,' observed Jeff. 'I say hard luck for you and Dr Thackery, you'd have been on your way by now.' He grinned. 'What a way to see the New Year in!'

Clotilde was far too busy to know exactly when midnight struck. The night staff had come on duty hours ago, she had sent her own nurses off, and with the promise of a relief as soon as it could be arranged, was toiling on with occasional help from the senior night runner and one of the Night Sisters when she could spare the time. James and Jeff and Mr Pratt were still there, disappearing every now and then to go to Men's Medical, although there were fewer patients admitted there. It was well after midnight before a relief staff nurse took over from Clotilde and since there was no sign of James, she went off duty, to fall into bed to sleep like a log until the morning. She had forgotten all about New Year.

It seemed to her that she was going on duty again in no time at all; she responded to the 'Happy New Year' greetings from everyone she encountered, intent on getting to the ward to see how the rest of the night had gone.

Not nearly so badly, as it turned out. The unfortunate victims of the wedding feast were wan and pale, but no longer suffering their distressing symptoms with such frequency. They were all drinking any fluids they fancied and except for the last two to be admitted, were off their drips.

'I only have to turn my back,' remarked Sally. 'It must have been bedlam, Sister. And of course you didn't get off duty ... wasn't there anyone to relieve you?'

'Not until after midnight,' Clotilde sighed gently. 'I

didn't dare take my days off . . . I'll have them later in the week. I should think most of these poor souls will go home tomorrow—a fluid diet and a day's rest should put them back on their feet.'

An opinion substantiated by James when he returned during the morning. All but two of them would be able to leave on the following day, and those two would have to remain until he was satisfied they had fully recovered.

Clotilde, dispensing coffee, had little to say for herself beyond strictly professional replies to his queries, but as they got up to leave the ward, James said casually: 'I've arranged for you to have your days off on the day after tomorrow, Clotilde—I'll be at the entrance about eight o'clock. We can stop for breakfast as we go.'

It was difficult—impossible—to give any kind of a coherent answer with Jeff and Sally and Mr Pratt all staring at her. In any case, James didn't appear to expect one. He said very formally: 'Good day to you, Sister Collins,' and strode off to Men's Medical.

Clotilde spent her day vacillating between a delightful excitement and annoyance at the way he had arranged everything without even consulting her. And she still wasn't sure—he hadn't said he loved her, although she had to admit that he hadn't had the time for that, but surely he could have given a hint? He had kissed her, but he had done that before without apparently meaning a thing. She had no appetite, glancing up each time the door opened, keeping her mind on her work only by the greatest efforts. She went off duty that evening hoping there would be a message for her or that she might meet him on her way over to the home, but there was nothing. She washed her hair and went to supper and declared that she was tired enough to go to bed early, but not as early as she would have wished. The grapevine had done its work, and she was besieged by questions from her friends as to where she was going and why she was leaving. She answered them all with a calm she wasn't feeling and went at last to bed, where she lay awake for a long time, consumed by love for James and exasperation at his behaviour. And just supposing it's not me after all, she thought in sudden panic, and he's only being friendly because Katrina wants me to go and see her? She rehearsed the conversation they might be expected to have on their drive, thinking up the kind of remarks which would let him see that for her part, everything was very lighthearted. She fell asleep at last, her head in a fine muddle.

She had given herself a morning off duty and she spent the hour or so after breakfast packing an overnight bag—slacks and a thick sweater, a pretty dress for the evening and the things to go with it. She would travel in her suit and take her winter coat, because it was bitterly cold. That done, she went down to the phone box in the hall and phoned Rosie, who came on the line wanting to know if she was all right; there had been no letter and she hadn't rung up.

'I'm sorry, Rosie,' declared Clotilde. 'We had a lot of patients in with food poisoning and there wasn't time to do anything very much but look after them. Rosie, you knew about James buying the house?'

'Yes, love. Swore me to secrecy, he did, bless him. It was to be a nice surprise for you. He's told you, then?'

'Two days ago. Rosie, why did he do it?'

She heard a rich chuckle. 'You ask him that, Miss Tilly!'

'Well, I will. He's driving me down to his parents' home tomorrow morning—his sister has invited me. I'll come home next week—at least, I will if James hasn't moved in.' There was silence at the other end and she said quite sharply: 'Rosie, did you hear me?'

'Yes, love. I'll have a nice meal ready for you. Tinker will be ever so glad to see you.'

The ward had settled down quite well. The ladies who were to go home were up and dressed and enjoying a good gossip about their unfortunate experience and the rest of the patients were well enough to listen avidly. Clotilde, going about her day's work, paused to listen and sympathise and give advice, before leading Mr Pratt, still a bit out of his depth, up and down the ward, waiting patiently, which took a while, as he examined charts, read notes and made great play with his stethoscope. It was after lunch, when the ward was quiet and everyone had been settled in beds or on chairs to rest, and she was alone with a student nurse, as James came in. He walked quite quietly, not disturbing the patients, whispered something to the nurse and swept Clotilde into her office.

'I was about to tell you why circumstances are in my favour,' he said without preamble, popping her into her chair and sitting down on the desk in front of her. He picked up her hand and held it gently, stroking her wrist with his thumb. 'Most of them are unimportant, the one that matters is that at last you've realised that you're in love with me. It took a long time, didn't it, darling heart? I was beginning to fear I was to be cast in the role of an old friend for the rest of our lives.'

She looked at him shyly. 'How ever did you know?'

'I think I understand you better than you do yourself. Besides, I've loved you for a long time now—long before Bruce appeared on the scene. Being in love with someone makes one very perceptive.'

He stood up and plucked her out of her chair and pulled her into his arms. His kiss was more than satisfactory, it was a pity that the phone rang, and since it went on ringing, Clotilde disentangled herself and answered it.

It was for James. She handed him the phone and he kept an arm round her while he listened. 'I'll be over at once. You did quite right to tell me.' He put the phone down. 'Young Pratt, worried about a bronchiectasis on Men's Medical. My darling, I would like above all things to take you out for a meal this evening. But I've got several private patients to see between six and eight o'clock and a meeting at nine o'clock.' He kissed her hard. 'Don't be late in the morning or I shall come and fetch you!'

After he'd gone, Clotilde sat down at her desk, staring dreamily at the wall opposite her. There were so many questions to ask him and she hadn't remembered one of them, but it really didn't matter.

She was up early, taking great pains with her face and hair, making a cup of tea in the little pantry on the Sister's floor and then going down to the entrance. It was barely eight o'clock, but James was there. He settled her beside him, kissed her briefly, told her she looked beautiful and turned the Bentley's nose westward. There wasn't too much traffic. They were free of the suburbs and on the M3, sitting in a companionable silence until James said: 'Breakfast, darling. We'll stop at the next Happy Eater or service station unless we're lucky enough to find something open.'

They were—a small wayside hotel with a large notice

in the window offering breakfast. They ate their way
through bacon and eggs and toast and marmalade and
emptied the coffee pot, sitting in a pleasant little room
with an open fire. They didn't talk much; it was just as
though they were waiting for the right moment to
begin, just being with each other was enough for the
time being, thought Clotilde contentedly, and smiled at
James across the table.

'I want to say so much, but I don't know where to
start,' she told him, 'and somehow the motorway
doesn't seem the right place, so I don't want to start.'

He smiled tenderly at her. 'We'll find the right place,'
he assured her.

They took the A30 presently, the rather bleak road
from Salisbury until they reached the outskirts of
Shaftesbury. It had been snowing, and the view of white
fields below and around the town was beautiful. James
drove slowly into the narrow busy High Street, then
eased the car into a narrower lane to the left. There
were a handful of cottages on one side and at the end
large wooden gates open. He drove through them and
followed a drive round the back of an imposing
Regency house, to stop on the sweep before its front
door. He opened her door and took her arm. 'Home,'
he said. 'But before we go in come and see the view.'

There was a low wall beyond a stretch of lawn, and a
heavy wrought iron door in it. He didn't open it, but
stood looking through it at the magnificent sweep of
land below them. 'This is the right place,' he said. 'No
phone, no one to interrupt, just the two of us, my
dearest darling heart.' He caught her close, looking
down at her happy face and then kissing it, taking his
time. 'Will you marry me, my love? Just as soon as we
can arrange it. So much time wasted ... We'll have to

live in London, but we'll go to Wendens Ambo each weekend, and drive down here whenever we want a break. The children will like it . . .'

Clotilde said: 'I haven't said I'll marry you yet, and here we are with a family of lively children!' Her smile was quite beautiful.

James hugged her so close that her ribs ached. 'Marry me, my dearest?' he asked, and his voice was no longer placid.

She reached up to kiss him. 'There's nothing else in this world I'd rather do,' she told him. 'I can't think why I didn't discover that I loved you; three solid years of seeing you twice a week. I'm sorry I've wasted so much of your time,' she said meekly, 'waiting for me . . .'

'I'll see that you make up for it. Dear heart . . .' James paused and turned his head towards the house behind them. Even at this distance they could hear voices and dogs barking. The front door was flung wide and several people came on to the porch while the dogs came tearing across the lawn.

'Come and meet the family,' invited James, and put a great arm around her shoulders. It would be there, metaphorically speaking, cherishing her for the rest of their lives, thought Clotilde, walking beside him towards the house.